"I guess the joke was on me, wasn't it, Jesse?"

Jesse stood so close that she could feel the heat of his body. "Damn it, Glory, what are you talking about?"

Her control snapped. "My God," she spat, all pain and fury. "I hate you for keeping her from me like that!"

His hands came to rest on her shoulders, and their weight and strength had a steadying effect. "I get the feeling that you're talking about Liza," he said. "What I don't get is why she's any of your concern."

Her tears shimmered along her lashes, blurring his features. "Liza's my daughter," she sobbed. "Mine and yours."

He let her go and turned away, and she couldn't see into his eyes or read the expression on his face.

"That's a lie," he said, his tone so low she could barely hear him.

Also available from MIRA Books and
LINDA LAEL MILLER

STATE SECRETS
USED-TO-BE LOVERS
JUST KATE
ONLY FOREVER
DARING MOVES
MIXED MESSAGES

Coming soon

THERE AND NOW

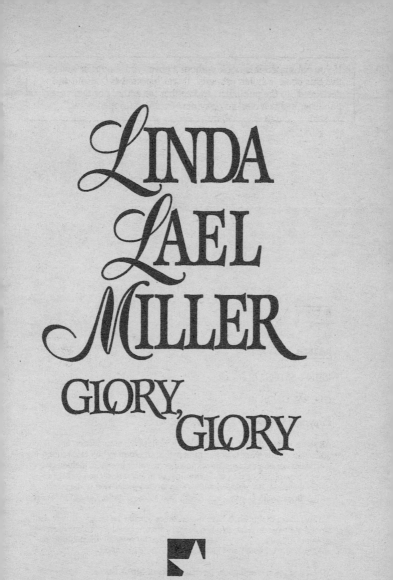

LINDA LAEL MILLER

GLORY, GLORY

MIRA BOOKS

ISBN 1-55166-179-9

GLORY, GLORY

For Betty Wojcik, a friend indeed.
Thanks for everything.

1

Glory Parsons's gloved hands tightened on the steering wheel when the familiar green-and-white sign came into view. *Pearl River, Oregon. Population: 6710.*

All it would take was one U-turn, and she could be headed back toward Portland. She'd find another job, and she still had her apartment. Maybe she and Alan could work things out....

She swallowed hard. She would be in Pearl River three weeks at the outside, then she could join her friend Sally in San Francisco, get a new job and start her life all over again. As for Alan, she hoped his teeth would fall out.

The feed store was festooned in lights and sparkling green garlands for Christmas, like the five-and-dime and the bookstore and the newspaper office. The street was thick with muddy slush, but fat puffs of new snow were falling.

Glory passed the diner and smiled to see the cheap plastic Santa and reindeer perched on the tarpaper roof. She touched her horn once, in a preliminary greeting to her mother, and drove on.

The cemetery was on the other side of town, overlooking the river. Glory parked outside the gates, behind a green police car, and made her way up the curving driveway. She left her purse in the car, carrying a bouquet of holly she'd picked along the roadside earlier in the day.

A crisp breeze riffled the drifting snowflakes and Glory's chin-length silver-gold hair. She pulled up the collar of her long woolen coat, royal blue to match her eyes, and made her way carefully along a slippery walk.

Dylan's grave lay beneath a white blanket of snow, and Glory's throat thickened when she came to stand beside it. "Hi, handsome," she said hoarsely, stooping to put the holly into the metal vase at the base of his headstone. Her eyes filled with tears, and she wedged both hands deep into her coat pockets and sniffled. "You had your nerve, dying at twenty-two. Don't you know a girl needs her big brother?"

She dusted snow from the face of the stone, uncovering Dylan's name and the dates of his birth and death. He'd perished in an explosion soon after joining the air force, and Glory didn't want anyone to forget he'd lived, even for the space of an afternoon snowfall.

She drew a deep breath and dried her eyes with the back of one hand. "I swore I'd never come back here," she went on miserably, "even to see you. But Mama's getting married, so I had to come to her wedding." She took a tissue from her pocket and dabbed at her nose. "I got myself hooked up with a real jerk back in Portland, Dylan. If you'd been around, you probably would have punched him in the mouth. He pretended to love me, and then he stole my promotion right out from under me."

She paused to look up at the cloudy sky. The bare limbs of maple and elm trees seemed to splinter it.

"I quit my job and had my furniture put in storage," Glory confided to her brother, gazing at the marble headstone again. "And after Christmas and Mama's wedding, I'm going to San Francisco to make a life for myself. I don't know when I'll be back to see you again."

A swishing sound in the slush alerted Glory to someone's approach. She looked up, and her blue eyes went wide.

"Jesse."

He was standing on the other side of Dylan's grave, dressed in the standard green-and-brown uniform of the sheriff's department. He wore no hat, and his badge, pinned to his jacket, gleamed in the thin winter light. Like Glory, he was twenty-eight years old.

His caramel eyes moved over her frame then swept back to her face. "What are you doing here?" he asked, as though he'd caught her in a bank vault after-hours.

Glory had known she couldn't come back to Pearl River without encountering Jesse—she just hadn't expected it to happen this soon. Her temper flared, along with an old ache in a corner of her heart she'd long since closed off, and she gestured toward Dylan's headstone. "What do you think I'm doing here?" she retorted. "I came to see my brother."

Jesse hooked his thumbs through the loops on his trousers, and his brazen brown eyes narrowed slightly. "It's been eight years since the funeral. You were really anxious to get back."

Eight years since the funeral, eight years since Glory had laid eyes on Jesse Bainbridge.

Pride forced Glory to retaliate. She took in his uniform and then said, "I see you've been promoted to sheriff. Did your grandfather buy the election?"

His jawline tightened for a moment, but then he grinned in that wicked way that had broken so many hearts in high school. "Why not? He bought you, didn't he?" Like everyone else in Pearl River,

Jesse probably believed old Seth Bainbridge had paid her to leave town; Glory was fairly certain he'd never learned about the baby.

Without waiting for a reply, Jesse settled his hat on his head and walked away.

Glory barely resisted the urge to scoop up a handful of snow and hurl it at his back. Only the awareness of where she was kept her from doing just that.

When Jesse was out of earshot, Glory put her hands on her hips and told Dylan, "He really burns me up. I don't know why you liked him so much."

You liked him, too, she heard Dylan's voice say, way down deep in her heart. *You had his baby, Glory.*

"Don't remind me!" Glory snapped, folding her arms. "I was barely eighteen, and my hormones were out of control!"

She thought she heard Dylan's laughter in the chilly winter breeze, and in spite of the unpleasant encounter with Jesse Bainbridge a few minutes before, she smiled.

"I love you, Dylan," she said, touching the headstone again. Then, with her hands in her pockets, she turned and made her way down the walk to the driveway and the towering wrought-iron gates.

It was time to face Pearl River, something she hadn't done since Dylan's funeral, and she was reluctant for more than one reason.

Glory's sports car, the one great extravagance in her life, started with a comforting roar, and she drove slowly back into town, telling herself to take things one moment at a time. Before she knew it, Christmas and the New Year's wedding would be over, and she could get on with her life.

She parked in front of Delphine's Diner just before an orange snowplow came past, flinging a picturesque fan of slush at the sidewalk. Glancing up at the life-size plastic Santa and reindeer, Glory remembered Dylan sliding around on the roof to put them in place for Christmases past, deliberately clowning because he knew his mother and sister were afraid he'd fall.

The little bell over the door jingled when Glory went inside. Her mother, as slender and active as ever, lit up brighter than the Santa over their heads when she saw her daughter.

"Glory," she whispered with a choked sob of pleasure. And then she was hurrying across the brown-and-white linoleum floor, with its swirls of fresh wax, to embrace her.

The hug brought a lump to Glory's throat and quick tears to her eyes. "Hello, Mama."

"It's about time you got here," boomed a male voice from one of the stools at the counter. Harold Seemer, the good-natured plumbing contractor who had finally persuaded Delphine to marry him after a five-year courtship, beamed at his future step-daughter. "We were about to send the sheriff's patrol out after you."

Glory tried not to react visibly to the indirect mention of Jesse. She didn't want thoughts of him interfering with her visit. "Hi, Harold," she said, giving the well-fed balding man a hug. He and Delphine had visited her in Portland on several occasions, and she'd become very fond of him.

"You look skinny," Delphine commented, narrowing her green eyes as Glory took off her coat and hung it on one of the chrome hooks beside the door.

Glory laughed. "Thanks, Mama. I've been dieting for two months to make up for all the food you're going to force me to eat."

Harold finished his coffee and replaced the beige china cup in its saucer, with a clink. "Well, I've got to get back to work. I'll leave you two to catch up on everything."

When he was gone, Glory took a stool at the counter, sighed, and pushed back her hair. "No customers," she commented, looking around at the six Formica-topped tables. The chrome legs of the chairs glistened, and so did the red vinyl seats.

Delphine shrugged and, stepping behind the counter, poured a cup of coffee to set in front of her daughter. "The lunch crowd's been and gone. Things'll be quiet until dinnertime."

Glory reached for her cup and saucer and pulled them toward her, feeling the steam caress her face and taking comfort in the familiar aroma, but she didn't drink. "I saw Jesse," she said, and her voice was shaky.

"Did you, now?" Delphine's voice was light as the feathery snow falling past the window with its neon "We Serve Pepsi-Cola" sign. "How did that happen?"

"I stopped by the cemetery to leave some holly for Dylan, and he was there." Glory raised her eyes, watched her mother's face pale slightly at the mention of her lost son. But Delphine recovered her composure rapidly, like always. She was nothing if not a survivor.

"Jesse's brother, Gresham, is buried there, along with his sister-in-law, Sandy, and his folks. Must be some special day to him, or something."

Glory recalled the plane crash that had taken the lives of Gresham Bainbridge, promising young state senator, and his pretty wife, Sandy. The tragedy had been big news in Oregon. "They left a child behind, didn't they?'' Glory asked, because think-ing about the Bainbridges' misfortune was better than remembering her own and Delphine's.

Delphine busied herself rinsing out a glass pot and starting a new batch of decaffeinated coffee brewing. "A little girl," she said quietly. After a few more moments, she turned to face her daugh-ter, leaning against the spotless counter, her shrewd eyes inviting—even demanding—confidences. "Tell me about this Alan man. What did he do that made you uproot yourself like that?"

Glory ran her tongue over her lips and fiddled with a paper napkin. She still hadn't touched her coffee. "He was a rat, Mama," she answered after a long time. "He cozied up to all my clients while I was away taking a training course in Chicago, and when I came home, the board had given him the promotion they promised me."

"So you just threw your resignation in their faces, cleared out your desk and left?" Delphine put the question in a nonchallenging way, but it still made Glory's cheeks flame.

And she definitely felt defensive. "What should I have done, Mama? Stayed and brought Alan pencils and files in my teeth? I worked night and day for *four years* to earn that job!"

Delphine shrugged, leaning on the counter again. "I think maybe you just wanted out of the relationship and that was the best excuse that occurred to you. In fact, I wouldn't be surprised to learn that you've never gotten over Jesse Bainbridge."

Glory's hands shook as she picked up the coffee and took an angry gulp. It burned her tongue and the roof of her mouth. "Well, I have!" she sputtered moments later. It still hurt that Jesse hadn't come for her at the unwed-mothers' home in Portland and brought her home to have their baby, even though she knew the scenario was woven of pure fantasy. Jesse couldn't have come for her because he hadn't known she was pregnant. "It was nothing but a childish high-school infatuation in the first place."

Delphine's eyes took on a sad look. "It was more than that," she insisted softly, resting one well-manicured hand on Glory's arm.

Glory pulled away, went to the jukebox and busied herself studying the titles of the songs imprisoned inside. They were all old tunes she couldn't bear to hear when her feelings were so raw.

She turned to the window instead.

Mr. Kribner came out of the drugstore across the street and hung an evergreen wreath on his front door.

"Merry Christmas," Glory muttered, wishing she'd never left Portland. She could have made some excuse for the holidays, then dashed into town for the wedding and out again after the reception.

Her mother's hands gripped her elbows firmly. "You're tired, sweetheart, and I'll bet you didn't have any lunch. Let me fix you something, and then you can go upstairs and rest a while."

Glory nodded, even though she had no appetite and hadn't really rested for days. She didn't want Delphine to worry about her, especially during this happy time, with the wedding and the holidays coming up.

"Harvey Baker was just in the other day," Delphine called sunnily from the kitchen, as Glory stood hugging herself and watching the snow swirl lazily past the diner windows. When it got dark, the Pepsi sign would make a pink glow on the white ground. "He's looking for an assistant over at the bank, you know. Allie Cordman left to take a job in Seattle."

"Smart girl," Glory murmured. Pearl River was a nowhere town, with nothing to offer. Anybody who deliberately made his home here ought to have his head examined.

Delphine hummed in the kitchen, happy with her world, and for one difficult moment Glory envied her profoundly. She wondered what it was like to be in love with a man she could trust and depend on, and to be loved by him in return.

Presently, Glory's favorite lunch—a clubhouse sandwich with potato salad—appeared on the counter, along with a tall diet cola with extra ice.

Glory would have sworn she wasn't hungry, but her stomach grumbled as she got back onto the stool and pulled a fresh napkin from the holder. "Thanks, Mama," she said.

Delphine was busy wiping the already immaculate counter. "There's an old-movie festival at the Rialto tonight," she told Glory cheerfully. "Jimmy Stewart in *It's a Wonderful Life* and Cary Grant in *The Bishop's Wife*."

A poignant sensation of nostalgia came over Glory. "Jimmy Stewart and Cary Grant," she sighed. "They don't make men like that anymore."

Delphine's green eyes twinkled, and she flashed her diamond engagement ring. "Don't be too sure," she said coyly, and Glory laughed.

"Mama, you're hopeless!" But she couldn't help thinking, as she ate her sandwich and tangy potato salad, that it would be nice to have a handsome angel turn up in her life, the way Cary Grant had appeared in Loretta Young's.

Two teenage boys came in, raising a great ruckus lest they go unnoticed, and plunked quarters into the jukebox. A lively old Christmas rock tune filled the diner, and they piled into chairs at one of the tables.

Suddenly wanting to relive her after-school waitress days in that very diner, Glory abandoned her sandwich and reached for a pencil and an order pad.

"What'll it be, guys?" she asked.

The young men ran appreciative eyes over her trim blue jeans and gray cashmere sweater.

"Will you marry me?" asked the one with braces.

Glory laughed. "Sure. Just bring a note from your mother."

The other boy hooted at that, and the first one blushed. The name on the sleeve of his letter-man's jacket was Tony.

"I want a cheeseburger, a vanilla shake and an order of curly fries," he said, but the look in his eyes told Glory he had bigger things in mind than food.

Glory was writing the order down when the bell over the door jingled. She looked up to see Jesse dusting snow off his shoulders onto Delphine's clean floor.

His gaze skirting Glory as though she'd suddenly turned invisible, he greeted the boys by name and took a place at the counter. "Hi, Delphine," he said, as the woman poured his coffee. "How's my best girl?"

Glory concentrated fiercely on the second boy's order, and when she'd gotten it, she marched into the kitchen and started cooking. She had to keep herself busy—and distracted—until Jesse finished his coffee and left the diner.

"What's he doing here?" she whispered to her mother, when Delphine joined her to lift the basket out of the deep fryer and shake the golden fries free of grease.

Delphine smiled. "He's drinking coffee."

Glory glowered at her. "I'm going upstairs!" she hissed.

"That'll fix him," Delphine said.

In a huff, Glory took the cheeseburgers off the grill and the shakes off the milk-shake machine. She made two trips to the boys' table and set everything down with a distinctive *clunk*. All the while, she studiously ignored Jesse Bainbridge.

He'd just come in to harass her, she was sure of that. He probably bullied everybody in Pearl River, just like his grandfather always had.

The jukebox took a break, then launched into a plaintive love song. Glory's face was hot as she went back to the kitchen, hoping Jesse didn't remember how that tune had been playing on the radio the first time they'd made love, up at the lake.

She couldn't help glancing back over one shoulder to see his face, and she instantly regretted the indulgence. Jesse's bold brown eyes glowed with the memory, and his lips quirked as he struggled to hold back a smile.

Glory flushed to recall how she'd carried on that long-ago night, the pleasure catching her by surprise and sending her spiraling out of her small world.

"That does it," she muttered. And she stormed out to her car, collected her suitcase and overnighter, and marched up the outside stairs to her mother's apartment.

The moment she stepped through the door, Glory was awash in memories.

The living room was small and plain, the furniture cheap, the floor covered in black-and-beige linoleum tiles. A portable TV with foil hooked to the antenna sat on top of the old-fashioned console stereo.

Glory put down her luggage, hearing the echoes of that day long, long before, when Delphine had taken a job managing the diner downstairs. Dylan had been fourteen then, Glory twelve, and they'd all been jubilant at the idea of a home of their own. They'd lived out of Delphine's old rattletrap of a car all summer, over at the state park next to the river, but the fall days were getting crisp and the nights were downright cold.

Besides, Delphine's money had long since run out, and they'd been eating all their meals in the church basement, with the old people and the families thrown out of work because of layoffs at the sawmill.

Dylan and Glory had slept in bunk beds provided by the Salvation Army, while Delphine had made her bed on the couch.

Pushing the door shut behind her, Glory wrenched herself back to the present. It was still too painful to think about Dylan twice in one day, even after all the time that had passed.

Glory put her baggage in the tiny bedroom that was Delphine's now, thinking that she really should have rented a motel room. When she'd suggested it on the telephone, though, her mother had been adamant: Glory would stay at the apartment, and it would be like old times.

She paced, too restless to unpack or take a nap, but too tired to do anything really demanding. After peeking out the front window, past the dime-store wreath with the plastic candle in it, to make sure Jesse's car was gone, she went back downstairs for her coat.

The cook who took Delphine's place at two-thirty had arrived, along with a teenage waitress and a crowd of noisy kids from the high school.

Delphine handed Glory her coat, then shrugged into her own. "Come on," she said, pushing her feet into transparent plastic boots. "I'll show you the house Harold and I are going to live in."

The snow fell faster as the two women walked along the familiar sidewalk. Now and then, Delphine paused to wave at a store clerk or a passing motorist.

They rounded a corner and entered an attractive development. The houses had turrets and gable windows, though they were modern, and the yards were nicely landscaped.

Glory remembered playing in this part of town as a child. There had been no development then, just cracked sidewalks that meandered off into the deep grass. The place had fascinated her, and she'd imagined ghost houses lining the walks, until Dylan had spoiled everything by telling her there had been Quonset huts there during World War II to accommodate workers at the town smelter.

Delphine stopped to gaze fondly at a charming little mock colonial with a snow-dusted rhododendron bush growing in the yard. The house itself was white, the shutters dark blue. There were flower boxes under all the windows.

Glory's eyes widened with pleasure. This was the kind of house her mother had always dreamed of having. "This is it?" she asked, quite unnecessarily.

Proudly Delphine nodded. "Harold and I signed the papers on Friday. It's all ours."

Impulsively, Glory hugged her mother. "You've come a long way, baby!" she said, her eyes brimming with happy tears.

Both of them stood still in the falling snow, remembering other days, when even in their wildest dreams neither of them would have dared to fantasize about owning a house such as this one.

"Are you going to keep the diner?" Glory asked, linking her arm with Delphine's as they walked back toward the center of town.

Delphine's answer came as no surprise. After all, she'd worked and scrimped and sacrificed to buy the place from her former employers. "Of course I am. I wouldn't know what to do if I couldn't go down there and make coffee for my customers."

With a chuckle, Glory wrapped her arm around her mother's straight little shoulders. "I imagine they'd all gather in your kitchen at home, they're so used to telling you their troubles over a steaming cup."

Back at the apartment, Delphine immediately excused herself, saying she had to "gussy up" for the Stewart-Grant festival at the Rialto.

"Sure you don't want to come along?" she queried, peering around the bathroom door, her red hair falling around her face in curls. "Harold and I would be glad to have you."

Glory shook her head, pausing in her unpacking. "I feel as though parts of me have been scattered in every direction, Mama. I need time to gather myself back together. I'll get something light for supper, then read or watch TV."

Delphine raised titian eyebrows. "You're getting boring in your old age, kid," she said. "Just see that you don't eat over at Maggie's. Last week one of the telephone linemen told me he got a piece of cream pie there that had dust on top of it."

"I wouldn't think of patronizing your archrival, Mama," Glory replied, grinning. "Even though I do think serving pie with dust on it requires a certain admirable panache."

Delphine dismissed her daughter with a wave and disappeared behind the bathroom door.

As it happened, Glory bought spaghetti salad in the deli at the supermarket and ate it while watching the evening news on the little TV with the foil antenna. Downstairs in the diner, the dinner hour was in full swing, and the floor vibrated with the blare of the jukebox.

Glory smiled and settled back on the couch that would be her bed for the next several weeks, content.

She was home.

After the news was over, however, the reruns of defunct sitcoms started. Glory flipped off the TV and got out her mother's photo albums. As always, they were tucked carefully away in the record compartment of the console stereo, along with recordings by Roy Orbison, Buddy Holly, Ricky Nelson and Elvis Presley.

Delphine probably hadn't looked at the family pictures in years, but Glory loved to pore over them.

Still, she had to brace herself to open the first album—she was sitting cross-legged on the couch, the huge, cheaply bound book in her lap—because she knew there would be pictures of Dylan.

He smiled back at her from beside a tall man wearing a slouch hat. Glory knew the man's name had been Tom, and that he'd been mean when he drank. He'd also been her father, but she didn't remember him.

The little boy leaning against his leg, with tousled brown hair and gaps in his grin, was another matter. Gently, with just the tip of one finger, Glory touched her brother's young face.

"When am I going to get over missing you, Bozo?" she asked, in a choked voice, using the nickname that had never failed to bug him.

Glory stared at Dylan for a few more moments, then turned the page. There she made her first photographic appearance—she was two months old, being bathed in a roasting pan on a cheap tabletop, and her grin was downright drunken.

She smiled and sighed. "The body of a future cheerleader. Remarkable."

Her journey through the past continued until she'd viewed all the Christmases and Halloweens, all the birthdays and first days of school. In a way, it eased the Dylan-shaped ache in her heart.

When she came to the prom pictures of herself and Jesse, taken in this very living room with Delphine's Kodak Instamatic, she smiled again.

Jesse was handsome in his well-fitting suit, while she stood proudly beside him in the froth of pink chiffon Delphine had sewn for her. The dress had a white sash, and she could still feel the gossamer touch of it against her body. Perched prominently above her right breast was Jesse's corsage, an orchid in the palest rose.

She touched the flat, trim stomach of the beaming blond girl in the picture. Inside, although Glory hadn't known it yet, Jesse's baby was already growing.

Glory closed the album gently and set it aside before she could start wondering who had adopted that beautiful little baby girl, and whether or not she was happy.

The next collection of pictures was older. It showed Delphine growing up in Albuquerque, New Mexico, and there were photographs of a collage of aunts, uncles and cousins, too.

Glory reflected as she turned the pages that it must have been hard for Delphine after she left another abusive husband. Her family had understood the first time, but they couldn't forgive a second mistake. And after Delphine fled to Oregon with her two children, she was virtually disowned.

Saddened, Glory turned a page. The proud, aristocratic young face of her Irish great-grandmother gazed out of the portrait, chin at an obstinate angle. Of all the photographs Delphine had kept, this image of Bridget McVerdy was her favorite.

In 1892, or thereabouts, Bridget had come to America to look for work and a husband. She'd been employed as a lowly housemaid, but she'd had enough pride in her identity to pose for this picture and pay for it out of nominal wages, and eventually she'd married and had children.

The adversities Bridget overcame over the years were legion, but Delphine was fond of saying that her grandmother hadn't stopped living until the day she died, unlike a lot of people.

Glory gazed at the hair, which was probably red, and the eyes, rumored to be green, and the proud way Bridget McVerdy, immigrant housemaid, held her head. And it was as though their two souls reached across the years to touch.

Glory felt stronger in that moment, and her problems weren't so insurmountable. For the first time in weeks, giving up didn't seem to be the only choice she had.

2

The next morning, after a breakfast of grapefruit, toast and coffee, Glory drove along the snow-packed streets of Pearl River, remembering. She went to the old covered bridge, which looked as though it might tumble into the river at any moment, and found the place where Jesse had carved their initials in the weathered wood.

A wistful smile curved Glory's lips as she used one finger to trace the outline of the heart Jesse had shaped around the letters. Underneath, he'd added the word, *Forever.*

"Forever's a long time, Jesse," she said out loud, her breath making a white plume in the frosty air. The sun was shining brightly that day, though the temperature wasn't high enough to melt the snow and ice, and the weatherman was predicting that another storm would hit before midnight.

A sheriff's-department patrol car pulled up just as Glory was about to slip behind the wheel of her own vehicle and go back to town. She was relieved to see that the driver wasn't Jesse.

The deputy bent over to roll down the window on the passenger side, and Glory thought she remembered him as one of the boys who used to orchestrate food fights in the cafeteria at Pearl River High. "Glory?" His pleasant if distinctly ordinary face beamed. "I heard you were back in town. That's great about your mom getting married and everything."

Glory nodded. She couldn't quite make out the letters on his identification pin. She rubbed her mittened hands together and stomped her feet against the biting cold. "Thanks."

"You weren't planning to drive across the bridge or anything, were you?" the deputy asked. "It's been condemned for a long time. Somebody keeps taking down the sign."

"I just came to look," Glory answered, hoping he wouldn't put two and two together. This had always been the place where young lovers etched their initials for posterity, and she and Jesse had been quite an item back in high school.

The lawman climbed out of his car and began searching around in the deep snow for the "condemned" sign. Glory got into her sports car, started the engine, tooted the horn in a companionable farewell, and drove away.

She stopped in at the library after that, and then the five-and-dime, where she and Dylan used to buy Christmas and birthday presents for Delphine. She smiled to recall how graciously their mother had accepted bottles of cheap cologne and gauzy handkerchiefs with stylized *D*'s embroidered on them.

At lunch time, she returned to the apartment, where she ate a simple green salad and half a tuna sandwich. The phone rang while she was watching a game show.

Eager to talk to anyone besides Alan or Jesse, Glory snatched up the receiver. "Hello?"

The answering voice, much to her relief, was female. "Glory? Hi, it's Jill Wilson—your former confidante and cheerleading buddy."

Jill hadn't actually been Glory's best friend— that place had belonged to Jesse—but the two had been close in school, and Glory was delighted at the prospect of a reunion. "Jill! It's wonderful to hear your voice. How are you?"

In the years since Dylan's funeral, Glory and Jill had exchanged Christmas cards and occasional phone calls, and once they'd gotten together in Portland for lunch. Time and distance seemed to drop away as they talked. "I'm fine—still teaching at Pearl River Elementary. Listen, is there any chance we could get together at my place for dinner tonight? I've got a rehearsal at the church at six, and I was hoping you could meet me there afterward. Say seven?"

"Sounds great," Glory agreed, looking forward to the evening. "What shall I bring?"

"Just yourself," Jill answered promptly. "I'll see you at First Lutheran tonight, then?"

"Definitely," Glory promised.

She took a nap that afternoon, since she and Jill would probably be up late talking, then indulged in a long, leisurely bubble bath. She was wearing tailored wool slacks in winter white, along with a matching sweater, when Delphine looked her up and down from the bedroom doorway and whistled in exclamation.

"So Jesse finally broke down and asked for a date, huh?"

Glory, who had been putting the finishing touches on her makeup in front of the mirror over Delphine's dresser, grimaced. "No. And even if he did, I'd refuse."

Delphine, clad in jeans and a flannel shirt for a visit to a Christmas-tree farm with Harold, folded her arms and assembled her features into an indulgent expression. "Save it," she said. "When Jesse came into the diner yesterday, there was so much electricity I thought the wiring was going to short out."

Glory fiddled with a gold earring and frowned. "Really? I didn't notice," she said, but she was hearing that song playing on the jukebox, and remembering the way her skin had heated as she relived every touch of Jesse's hands and lips.

"Of course you didn't," agreed Delphine, sounding sly. She'd raised one eyebrow now.

"Mother," Glory sighed, "I know you've been watching Christmas movies from the forties and you're in the mood for a good, old-fashioned miracle, but it isn't going to happen with Jesse and me. The most we can hope for, from him, is that he won't have me arrested on some trumped-up charge and run out of town."

Delphine shook her head. "Pitiful," she said.

Glory grinned at her. "This from the woman who kept a man dangling for five years before she agreed to a wedding."

Delphine sighed and studied her flawlessly manicured fingernails. "With my romantic history," she said, "I can't be too careful."

The two women exchanged a brief hug. "You've found the right guy this time, Mama," Glory said softly. "It's your turn to be happy."

"When does *your* turn come, honey?" Delphine asked, her brow puckered with a frown. "How long is it going to be before I look into your eyes and see something besides grief for your brother and that baby you had to give up?"

Glory's throat felt tight, and she turned her head. "I don't know, Mama," she answered, thinking of the word Jesse had carved in the wall of the covered bridge. *Forever.* "I just don't know."

Five minutes later, Glory left the apartment, her hands stuffed into the pockets of her long cloth coat. Since the First Lutheran Church was only four blocks away, she decided to walk the distance.

Even taking the long way, through the park, and lingering a while next to the big gazebo where the firemen's band gave concerts on summer nights, Glory was early. She stood on the sidewalk outside the church as a light snow began to waft toward earth, the sound of children's voices greeting her as warmly as the golden light in the windows.

Silent night, holy night
All is calm, all is bright...

Glory drew a breath cold enough to make her lungs ache and climbed the church steps. Inside, the music was louder, sweeter.

Holy Infant, so tender and mild...

Without taking off her coat, Glory slipped into the sanctuary and settled into a rear pew. On the stage, Mary and Joseph knelt, incognito in their twentieth-century clothes, surrounded by undercover shepherds, wise men and angels.

Jill, wearing a pretty plaid skirt in blues and grays, along with a blouse and sweater in complimentary shades, stood in front of the cast, her long brown hair wound into a single, glistening braid.

"That was fabulous!" she exclaimed, clapping her hands together. "But let's try it once more. Angels, you need to sing a little louder this time."

Glory smiled, brushing snow off her coat as Jill hurried to the piano and struck up an encore of "Silent Night."

The children, ranging in age from five or so to around twelve, fascinated Glory. Sometimes she regretted studying finance instead of education; as a teacher, she might have been able to make up, at least in a small way, for one of the two major losses in her life—she would have gotten to spend time around little ones. As it was, she didn't even *know* any kids—they just didn't apply for fixed-rate mortgages or car loans.

Joseph and Mary looked enough alike to be brother and sister, with their copper-bright hair and enormous brown eyes. Two of the wise men were sporting braces, and the third had a cast on his right arm.

Glory was trying to decide who was an angel and who was a shepherd when her gaze came to rest on a particular little girl. Suddenly she scooted forward in her seat and gripped the back of the next pew in both hands.

Looking back at her from beneath flyaway auburn bangs was the pretty, pragmatic face of Bridget McVerdy, Glory's great-grandmother.

For a moment the pews seemed to undulate wildly, like images in a fun-house mirror, and Glory rested her forehead against her hands. Almost a minute passed before she could be certain she wasn't going to faint.

"Glory?" A hand came to rest with gentle firmness on her shoulder. "Glory, are you all right?"

She looked up and saw Jill standing over her, green eyes filled with concern. Her gaze darted back to the child, and the interior of the church started to sway again. Unless Dylan had fathered a baby without ever knowing, or telling his mother and sister...

"Glory," Jill repeated, sounding really worried now.

"I—I'm fine," Glory stammered. She tried to smile, but her face trembled with the effort. "I just need some water—"

"You sit right there," Jill said in a tone of authority. "I'll get you a drink."

By the time she returned with a paper cup filled with cold water, Glory had managed to get back in sync with the earth's orbit, and the feeling of queasy shock in her stomach had subsided.

Talk about your forties movies and Christmas miracles, she thought, her eyes following the child that had to be her own.

Jill excused herself and looked at her watch as she walked up the aisle. Parents were starting to arrive, peering through the sanctuary doors and congregating in the back pews.

"All right, showstoppers," Jill said, "it's a wrap, for tonight, at least. Angels, practice your songs. You were a little rusty on 'It came upon a Midnight Clear.'"

Glory wondered if she'd be able to stand without her knees buckling. She fumbled through her purse for aspirin and took two tablets with what remained of her water.

Just then, the little girl on the stage broke away from the other angels and shepherds and came running down the aisle, grinning.

Glory's eyes widened as her daughter drew nearer and nearer, turned slightly in her seat to see her fling her arms around a man clad in blue jeans, boots and a sheepskin coat.

Jesse.

"Hi'ya, Munchkin," he said, bending to kiss the child where her rich, red-brown hair was parted.

Glory's mouth dropped open. He knew, she thought frantically. Then she shook her head.

He *couldn't* know; fate couldn't be that cruel. His grandfather wouldn't have told him, Dylan hadn't known the truth, though he might have guessed, and Delphine had been sworn to secrecy.

At that moment Jesse's maple-colored eyes found Glory's face. They immediately narrowed.

Glory felt no more welcome in the First Lutheran Church than she had in the cemetery the day before. She sat up a little straighter, despite the fact that she was in a state of shock, and maintained her dignity. Jesse might be sheriff, but that didn't give him the right to intimidate people.

He opened his mouth, then closed it again. After raising the collar of his macho coat, he turned his attention back to the child, ignoring Glory completely.

"Come on, Liza," he said, his voice sounding husky and faraway to Glory even though she could have reached out and touched the both of them. "Let's go."

Liza. Glory savored the name. Unable to speak, she watched Jesse and the child go out with the others. When she turned around again, Jill was kneeling backward in the pew in front of Glory's, looking down into her face.

"Feeling better?"

Glory nodded. Now that the initial shock had passed, a sort of euphoria had overtaken her. "I'll be fine."

Jill stood, shrugged into her plaid coat and reached for her purse. "Jesse's looking good, isn't he?"

"I didn't notice," Glory replied as the two women made their way out of the church. Jill turned out the lights and locked the front doors.

Her expression was wry when she looked into Glory's eyes again. "You were always a lousy liar, my friend. Some things never change."

Glory started to protest, then stopped herself. "Okay," she conceded, spreading her hands wide, as Jill led the way to a later-model compact car parked at the curb. She was too shaken to offer an argument, friendly or otherwise. "He looks terrific."

"They say he's never gotten over you."

Glory got into the car and snapped her seat belt in place. Strange, she'd spent the past eight years thinking about Jesse, but now a gangly child with auburn hair and green eyes was upstaging him in her mind. "The little girl—Liza. Where did she come from?"

Jill started the engine and smiled sadly before pulling out into traffic. "You remember Jesse's big brother, Gresham, don't you? He married Sandy Piper, from down at Fawn Creek. They couldn't have children, I guess, so they adopted Liza."

Glory let her head fall back against the headrest, feeling dizzy again. The car and Jill and even the snowy night all fell away like pages torn from a book, and suddenly Glory was eighteen years old again, standing in Judge Seth Bainbridge's imposing study....

She was pregnant, and she was scared sick.

The judge didn't invite her to take a chair. He didn't even look at her. He sat at his desk and cleaned out his pipe with a scraping motion of his penknife, speaking thoughtfully. "I guess you thought you and your mama and that brother of yours could live pretty high on the hog if you could just trap Jesse, didn't you?"

Glory clenched her fists at her sides. She hadn't even told Jesse about the baby yet, and she figured the judge only knew because he and Dr. Cupples were poker buddies. "I love Jesse," she said.

"So does every other girl between here and Mexico." At last, Jesse's grandfather raised sharp, sky-blue eyes to her face. "Jesse's eighteen years old. His whole life is ahead of him, and I won't see him saddled to some social-climbing little chippie with a bastard growing in her belly. Is that clear?''

The words burned Glory, distorted her soul like some intangible acid. She retreated a step, stunned by the pain. She couldn't speak, because her throat wouldn't open.

The judge sighed and began filling his pipe with fresh tobacco. The fire danced on the hearth, its blaze reflected in the supple leather of the furniture. ''I believe I asked you if I'd made myself clear, young lady.''

Glory swallowed hard. ''Clear enough,'' she got out.

The defiance he'd heard in her tone brought the judge's gaze slicing to Glory's face again. He and Jesse had a tempestuous relationship, but he obviously regarded himself as his grandson's protector. ''You'll go away to Portland and have that baby,'' he said. He waved one hand. ''For all I know, it could belong to any man in the county, but I'm taking you at your word that Jesse's the father. I'll meet all your expenses, of course, but you've got to do something in return for that. You've got to swear you'll never come back here to Pearl River and bother my grandson again.''

She was trembling from head to foot, though the room was suffocatingly warm. ''When I tell Jesse about the baby," she dared to say, "he'll want our child. And he'll want me, too."

Judge Bainbridge sighed with all the pathos of Job. "He's young and foolish, so you're probably right," the bitter old man concluded. He shook his head mournfully. "You leave me no choice but to drive a hard bargain, Missy. A very hard bargain, indeed."

Glory felt afraid, and she wished she hadn't been scared to tell Dylan about her pregnancy. He would have gotten mad all right, but then he'd probably have come with her to answer Judge Bainbridge's imperious summons. "What are you talking about?"

The most powerful man in all of Pearl River County smiled up at Glory from his soft leather chair. "Your brother—Dylan, isn't it? He's had a couple of minor scrapes with the law in recent months."

Glory's heart pounded to a stop, then banged into motion again. "It wasn't anything serious," she said, wetting her lips with a nervous tongue. "Just speeding. And he did tip over that outhouse on Halloween night, but there were others . . ."

Since Jesse had been one of those others, she left the sentence unfinished.

The judge lit his pipe and drew on the rich, aromatic smoke. He looked like the devil sitting there, presiding over hell, with the fire outlining his harsh features. "Dylan's about to go off to the air force and make something of himself," he reflected, as though speaking to himself. "But I guess they wouldn't want him if he were to be caught trying to break into a store or a house."

Glory felt the color drain from her face. Everybody knew Judge Bainbridge owned the sheriff and the mayor and the whole town council. If he wanted to, he could frame Dylan for anything short of murder and make it stick. "You wouldn't—Judge Bainbridge, sir, my brother doesn't have anything to do with—"

He chuckled and clamped down on the pipe stem with sharks' teeth. "So now I'm 'sir,' am I? That's interesting."

Glory closed her eyes and counted methodically, not trusting herself to speak. She was afraid she'd either become hysterical or drop to her knees and beg Jesse's grandfather not to ruin Dylan's chance to be somebody.

"You will leave town tomorrow morning on the ten o'clock bus," the judge went on, taking his wallet from the inside pocket of his coat and removing two twenty-dollar bills. "If you stay, or tell Jesse about this baby, your brother will be in jail, charged with a felony, before the week is out."

Glory could only shake her head.

Seth Bainbridge took up a pen, fumbled through a small metal file box for a card, and copied words and numbers onto the back of an envelope. "When you arrive in Portland, I want you to take a taxi to this address. My attorneys will take care of everything from there."

She was going to have to leave Jesse with no explanation, and the knowledge beat through the universe like a giant heartbeat. Just that day, out by the lake, they'd talked about getting married in late summer. They'd made plans to get a little apartment in Portland in the fall and start college together. Jesse had said his grandfather wouldn't like the idea, but he expected the old man to come around eventually.

All that had been before Glory's appointment with Dr. Cupples and the summons to Judge Bainbridge's study in the fancy house on Bayberry Road.

"I won't get rid of my baby," she said, lifting her chin. Tears were burning behind her eyes, but she would have died before shedding them while this monster of a man could see her.

Bainbridge's gaze ran over her once, from the top of her head to the toes of her sandals. "My lawyers will see that he or she is adopted by suitable people," he said. And with that he dismissed her.

"Glory?"

She was jerked back to the here and now as the car came to a lurching stop in Jill's slippery driveway. She peered through the windshield at a row of Georgian condominiums she'd seen that morning, while driving around and reacquainting herself with the town. There had been lots of changes in Pearl River over the last eight years; the sawmill was going at full tilt and the place was prosperous.

Jill strained to get her briefcase from the back seat and then opened the car door to climb out. "I know what you're thinking," she said. "You're wondering how I could afford a condo on a teacher's salary, aren't you?"

Actually Glory hadn't been wondering anything of the sort, but before she could say so, Jill went rushing on.

"Carl and I bought the place when we were married," she said, slamming her door as Glory got out to follow her inside. "When we got divorced, I kept the condo in lieu of alimony."

The evergreen wreath on Jill's front door jiggled as she turned the key in the lock and pushed.

"I guess that's fair—" Glory ventured uncertainly.

"Fair!" Jill hooted, slamming the door and kicking off her snow boots in the foyer. "I should hope so. After all, Carl makes five times as much money as I do."

Glory laughed and raised her hands in surrender. "I'm on your side, Jill. Remember?"

Jill smiled sheepishly, and after hanging up her coat and Glory's, led the way through the darkened living room and dining room to the kitchen. "I thought I'd make chicken stir-fry," she said, washing her hands at the sink.

"Sounds good," Glory replied. "Anything I can do to help?" She felt like a mannequin with a voice box inside. She said whatever was proper whenever a comment was called for. But her mind was on Liza, the little girl she'd been forced to surrender to a pack of expensive lawyers nine years before.

Jill shook her head and gestured toward the breakfast bar. "Have a seat on one of those stools and relax. I'll put water in the microwave for tea— or would you rather have wine?"

"Wine," Glory said, too quickly.

Although she didn't make a comment, Jill had definitely noticed Glory's strange behavior.

Nevertheless the two women enjoyed a light, interesting dinner. After a couple of hours of reminiscing, Glory asked Jill to take her back to the diner.

Glory didn't even pretend an interest in going upstairs to her mother's apartment. She plundered her purse for her keys and went from Jill's car straight to her own.

The sports car wasn't used to sitting outside on snowy nights, instead of in the warm garage underneath Glory's apartment complex, but it started after a few grinding coughs. Glory smiled and waved at Jill before pulling onto the highway and heading straight for the sheriff's office.

The same deputy Glory had encountered earlier that day—she saw now that his name tag said Paul Johnson—was on duty at the desk when she hurried in out of the cold.

It took all her moxy to make herself say, "I'd like to see Sheriff Bainbridge, please."

Deputy Johnson smiled, though not in an obnoxious way, and glanced at the clock. "He's gone home now, Glory."

Of course. Glory remembered that Jesse had been dressed in ordinary clothes when he'd come to the church to pick up Liza, instead of his uniform. "He still lives out on Bayberry Road, with his grandfather?" she asked, hoping she didn't sound like a crazy woman with some kind of fatal attraction.

The deputy plucked a tissue from a box on the corner of the desk and polished his badge with it. "The judge has been in a nursing home for five years now. His mind's all right, but he's had a couple of strokes, and he can't get around very well on his own."

Glory skimmed over that information. She couldn't think about Seth Bainbridge now, and she didn't want to take too close a look at her feelings about his situation. "But Jesse lives in the Bainbridge house?"

Officer Johnson nodded. "Yep." He braced his chubby hands on the edge of the desk, leaned forward, and said confidentially, "Adara Simms will be living out there with him soon enough, unless the missus and I miss our guess. Jesse's been dating her since she moved to town last year. 'Bout time they tied the knot."

Glory did her best to ignore the unaccountable pain this announcement caused her. She nodded and smiled and hurried back out to the parking lot.

The snow was coming down harder than before, and the wind blew it at a slant. The cold stung Glory's face and went right through her coat and mittens to wrap itself around her bones.

The downstairs windows of the big colonial house that had been in the Bainbridge family ever since Jesse's great-great-grandfather had founded the town of Pearl River glowed in the storm. Glory parked her car beside Jesse's late-model pickup truck and ran for the front porch.

She pounded the brass knocker against its base, then leaned on the doorbell for good measure.

"What the—" Jesse demanded, pulling a flannel shirt on over his bare chest even as he wrenched open the door. He was already wearing jeans and boots. "Glory," he breathed.

She resisted the temptation to peer around his shoulder, trying to see if the woman Deputy Johnson expected him to marry was around. "Is Liza here?" she asked evenly.

Grimacing against the icy wind, Jesse clasped Glory by one arm and wrenched her inside the house. "No," he said, on a long breath, after pushing the door closed. "I have legal custody of Liza, but she spends most of the time in town, with my cousin Ilene. I'm always getting called out in the middle of the night, and I don't want to leave her alone." He buttoned his shirt and shoved one hand self-consciously through his hair.

Jesse Bainbridge looked for all the world like a guilty husband caught in the wrong place at the wrong time.

Glory didn't care if she'd interrupted something. "Did you know?" she demanded, taking off her coat.

"Did I know what?" Jesse frowned, looking agitated again.

It was possible, of course, that he really hadn't learned who Liza was, or even that Glory had borne him a child, at all; but it seemed unlikely now. She wouldn't have been surprised to learn that Jesse and his grandfather had been in this together from the beginning.

"I guess the joke was on me, wasn't it, Jesse?" she said. Glory was amazed by her calm manner; inside, she was a raging tigress, ready to claw the man to quivering shreds.

He stood so close that she could feel the heat of his body. "Damn it, Glory, what the hell are you talking about?"

It was then that her control snapped, when she thought of all the Christmases and birthdays she'd missed, all the important occasions, like the appearance of the first tooth and the first faltering step. "God in heaven, Jesse," she spat, all pain and fury, "I hate you for keeping her from me like that!"

His hands came to rest on her shoulders, and their weight and strength had a steadying effect. So did the look of honest confusion in his dark eyes. "I get the feeling you're talking about Liza," he said evenly. "What I *don't* get is why she's any of your concern."

Glory's tears brimmed and shimmered along her lashes, blurring Jesse's features. "Liza's my daughter, damn you," she sobbed. "Mine and yours! I had her nine years ago in Portland, and your grandfather made me give her up!"

Jesse let her go and turned away, and she couldn't see into his eyes or read the expression on his face. "That's a lie," he said, his tone so low she could barely hear him.

3

Jesse walked into the mansion's massive living room, moving like a man lost in a fog, and sank into a leather chair. Glory followed, though he hadn't invited her, and took a seat on the bench in front of the grand piano, her arms folded.

She reminded herself that Jesse was a good actor. He'd been actively involved in the drama club in high school and probably college, too. Surely police work required an ability to disguise his emotions.

It would be no trick at all for him to pretend Liza's identity came as a surprise to him.

"Why didn't you tell me?" he asked, and his voice sounded hollow, raw.

Glory felt as though she'd been wound into a tight little coil. One slip, one wrong word, and she'd come undone in a spinning spiral. "Spare me the theatrics, Jesse," she said, wrapping her arms around her middle to hold herself in. "I know your grandfather let you in on his little secret a long time ago.''

Jesse pushed aside a tray on the coffee table containing the remains of a solitary frozen dinner, and swung his feet up onto the gleaming wood. He closed his eyes and rested his head against the back of the couch. ''This is crazy. Liza was Gresh and Sandy's child—they adopted her through some agency in California.''

Glory stood, shaking her head in angry wonder. ''You're incredible,'' she breathed, bolting from the piano bench and storming back out into the entry hall. Her coat had fallen off the brass tree, and she retrieved it from the floor.

She had one arm in the sleeve when Jesse gripped her by the shoulders and whirled her around.

''Just a minute, Glory,'' he told her, his brown eyes hot with golden sparks. ''You're not going to walk in here and announce that you had my baby and then waltz right out again. Furthermore, you'd better face the fact that Liza isn't that child.''

In that moment, Glory made up her mind to stay in Pearl River, even if she had to support herself by working at the diner, and become a part of Liza's life. She'd been forced to give her daughter up once, but she was a big girl now, and it was time she stopped letting people push her around.

Including Jesse.

"You can't get rid of me so easily this time, Jesse. I want to get to know Liza."

A myriad of emotions flickered in Jesse's eyes before he spoke again. "I didn't 'get rid' of you before," he said, his voice husky. "You left me, remember? Without even taking the trouble to say goodbye. My God, Glory, I looked *everywhere* for you. I begged your mother to tell me where you were, and Dylan and I got into three or four fights about it."

Glory didn't try to defend herself. She didn't have the strength. "Dylan couldn't have told you, Jesse, because he didn't know." She paused and sighed. "I guess you and I just didn't have whatever it takes."

She would have turned and walked out of the house then, but without an instant's warning, Jesse dragged her close and brought his mouth down on hers in a crushing kiss.

At first Glory was outraged, but as Jesse held her in place, his hands cupping her face, all the tumblers inside her fell into place and her heart swung open like the door of a safe. The old feelings rushed in like a tidal wave, washing away all the careful forgetting she'd done over the biggest part of a decade.

"Didn't we?" he countered harshly, when he finally let her go.

Glory was devastated to realize that Jesse still wielded the same treacherous power over her he had when they were younger. She'd been so certain that things had changed, that she was stronger and wiser now, but he had just proven that at least part of her independence was pure sham.

For all of it, she was still Jesse's girl.

She said a stiff goodbye and opened the door.

The snowstorm was raging and the wind caught Glory by surprise, pushing her back against the hard wall of Jesse's chest. She launched herself toward her car, and Jesse was right behind her.

"That glorified roller skate isn't going to get you back to town in this weather!" he bellowed. "Get into the truck!"

Glory considered ignoring his command until she got a glimpse of his face. The look in his eyes, coupled with the rising ferocity of the storm, effectively quashed her plans for a dramatic exit.

She let Jesse hoist her into his pickup truck and sat there shivering and hating herself while he ran back into the house for keys and a coat.

"Don't get the idea that this thing is settled," she warned, when he was behind the wheel, starting the engine and flipping switches to make the heater come on. The motor roared reassuringly, and Glory had to raise her voice. "Liza is my daughter, and

I'm not going to turn my back on her a second time.''

Jesse shifted the truck into reverse and clamped his teeth together for a moment before answering, ''I think it would be better if we talked about this tomorrow, when we're both feeling a little more rational.''

Glory folded her hands in her lap. She was overwrought, on the verge of screaming and crying. She desperately needed a night of sound sleep and some time to think. ''You're right,'' she said, hating to admit it.

''Well, glory be,'' Jesse marveled in a furious undertone, jamming the gearshift from first to second, and Glory ached inside. Once, he'd used that phrase in a very different way.

She bit down hard on her lower lip to keep from shouting at him for stealing all those minutes, hours, weeks and months when she could have been with Liza. And she wept as she thought of the things she'd missed.

When they finally reached the diner, Jesse got out of the truck and came around to help Glory down from the high running board. She pushed his hand aside, and suddenly she couldn't contain her anger any longer.

She stood staring up at him, her hands knotted in the pockets of her coat. ''You cheated me out of so many things," she said coldly. "First-grade pictures, Jesse. Dentist appointments and Halloween costumes and bedtime stories. You had no right!"

His hand crushed the lapels of her coat together, his strength raised her onto her tiptoes. "I loved you," he seethed. "I would have done anything for you, including break my back at the sawmill for the rest of my life to support you and our baby. I've been cheated out of a few things, too, Glory. I figure we're even."

With that, he released her and climbed back into the truck.

Glory grimaced as he sped away from the curb, his tires flinging slush in every direction and then screeching loudly on a patch of bare pavement.

Delphine was waiting up when Glory let herself into the apartment. A symmetrical five-foot Christmas tree stood in a corner of the living room, fragrant and undecorated.

"Was that Jesse?" Delphine asked without preamble.

Glory sighed. "Yes," she answered despondently, peeling off her gloves and coat and putting them away in a tiny closet.

"He sure had his shorts in a wad about something," Delphine commented, obviously fishing for more information.

"Sit down, Mama," Glory said wearily.

Delphine was sipping herb tea from a pretty china cup as she settled herself at one end of the sofa. "If you're going to tell me that Jesse was the father of your baby, Glory, save it. It's no flash."

Glory had a pounding headache, and she sat opposite her mother in a cheap vinyl chair, resting her elbows on her knees and rubbing both temples with her fingertips. "There's a lot more to it than that," she said wearily, wondering how to start. "Mama, you've lived here in Pearl River all this time. You must know about the child Jesse's brother and his wife adopted."

The teacup rattled against its saucer as Delphine set it on the coffee table. It was plain that she was making some calculations. "Yes," she said in an uncertain tone. "It was tragic when they died. Everybody said that plane crash brought on the judge's first stroke."

Glory nodded glumly. "Mama, the baby they adopted was mine." The tears she had been battling all evening welled up and trickled down her cheeks. "Jesse knew—that's the worst part. He sided with his grandfather."

"Are you sure about that?" Delphine frowned thoughtfully. "I'd have thought it would be more Jesse's style to hunt you down in Portland and confront you with the facts. He was shattered when you left, Glory—it was all I could do to keep myself from giving him the address of that home for unwed mothers you were staying in. He definitely wasn't buying my standard story that you were back East, living with my sister and attending a private school, but I think everybody else did."

Sniffling, Glory thrust herself out of her chair and went into the kitchenette for a paper towel. Her reflection showed in the window over the sink, and she could see that her mascara was smeared all over her face and her hair looked as if she'd just stuck one hand into a toaster.

She mopped her cheeks with the towel, not caring what she looked like, and went back to the living room. Seated in her chair again, she blew her nose vengefully. "You had a lot on your mind that summer, with me pregnant right out of high school and Dylan going off to the air force."

Delphine leaned forward slightly, her voice gentle. "Why didn't you want Dylan to know about the baby, Glory? We were a family—we shared everything."

Glory sighed. There was no point in keeping the secret any longer; Dylan couldn't be hurt by anything Judge Bainbridge or anyone else might do. "Because Jesse's grandfather said he'd have Dylan arrested for something serious, so the air force wouldn't take him. I was left with only one choice."

The color drained from Delphine's cheeks. "My God. Glory, why didn't you tell me all this *then*?"

"Because you would have told Dylan, and he'd have done something really stupid and gotten himself into even worse trouble."

Delphine reached across to clasp Glory's hand. "All of this is in the past," she said with a sigh and a resigned shrug. "What will you do now?"

Glory took a deep breath before answering, "I'm going to stay right here in Pearl River, so I can be near Liza."

"That might not be wise, dear," Delphine pointed out gently. "Liza's life will be turned upside down. She'll be terribly confused."

Shoving a hand through her rumpled hair, Glory sighed again. "I'm not going to tell her who I am, Mama," she said sadly. "I just want to be her friend."

Delphine rose off the old-fashioned couch and folded it down flat. "It's late, sweetheart," she said, disappearing into her bedroom for a few moments and returning with blankets, sheets and a pillow. "And you don't have to make any decisions tonight. Why don't you get some sleep?"

Together the two made up the bed, and Glory went into the bathroom to change into her nightgown, wash away her makeup, and brush her teeth.

When she returned, Delphine was waiting, perched on the arm of a chair.

"Glory, I know you've had a shock," she said quietly, "and I understand that your mind is in an uproar. But please don't forget how hard you worked to put yourself through school and build a fine career. Pearl River isn't going to be able to offer you what a big city could."

There was nothing Glory wanted more than to be close to her child. She would have lived in a metropolis or a remote Alaskan fishing village and given up any job. She kissed her mother's cheek without speaking, and Delphine went off to her room.

Glory got out the photo album and flipped to the page where Bridget McVerdy's picture was displayed. Sitting cross-legged in the middle of her couch bed, she touched the eternally youthful face and marveled. If she hadn't been one to pore over old family portraits, she'd never have suspected the truth about Gresham and Sandy Bainbridge's adopted daughter, even though it all seemed so obvious now.

After a long time, Glory set the album back in its place in the cabinet of her mother's old-fashioned stereo, switched out the lamp and crawled into bed.

Beyond the living-room windows, in the glow of the street lamps, transparent, silvery snow edged in gold drifted and swirled hypnotically.

Glory settled deeper into her pillow and yawned. Tomorrow she would pay a visit to Ilene Bainbridge, who ran a bookstore at the other end of Main Street. Glory had never met Ilene before, since, according to Delphine, the woman hadn't come to Pearl River to live until after the judge's first stroke.

Her mind drifted from the future to the past, back and back, to the night Liza was probably conceived. She and Jesse had gone to the lake for a moonlight picnic after the spring dance, and spread a blanket under a shimmering cottonwood tree....

The leaves above them caught the light of the moon and quivered like thousands of coins, and Jesse's dark eyes burned as he watched Glory take sparkling water, delicate sandwiches and fruit from the picnic basket. The surface of the lake was dappled with starlight, and soft music flowed from the radio of Jesse's flashy convertible.

He caught her wrist in one hand and pulled her to her feet to stand facing him on the blanket. "Dance with me," he said.

She'd already kicked off her high-heeled shoes. Laughing, Glory cuddled close to Jesse and raised her head for his kiss. He took her into his arms at the same time he was lowering his mouth to hers.

As always, Jesse's kiss electrified Glory. She didn't protest when he smoothed her white eyelet dress off her shoulders, his hands lightly stroking her skin as he bared it. She and Jesse meant to get married.

Glory's naked breasts glowed like the finest white opal when he uncovered them. The nipples hardened and reached for him, because they knew the pleasure Jesse could give.

"Glory be," he whispered in a strangled voice. "You're so beautiful it hurts to look at you."

She reached up with both hands to unpin her hair, and while her arms were raised, Jesse leaned forward and caught a coral-colored morsel between his lips.

Glory moaned and tried to lower her arms, but Jesse wouldn't let her. He closed one hand over both her wrists and held them firmly in place, and he gave as much pleasure as he took.

In the next few minutes, their clothes seemed to dissolve. Jesse lowered Glory gently to the blanket and stretched out beside her. While they kissed, his hand moved restlessly over her breasts and her taut stomach.

"Forever," he said breathlessly, his lips moving against the flesh of her neck. "I'll love you forever."

Jesse had long since taught Glory to desire him—their first encounter had taken place on that very spot just a few months before, and she didn't want to talk, not even about forever. Her young body was hungry, and she couldn't think beyond the moment.

"Make love to me, Jesse," she whispered, teasing him by nibbling at his lower lip, and he poised himself above her with a moan. She tasted his earlobe and kissed his neck, and when he entered her with a sudden, desperate thrust, she received him eagerly.

"Tell me you love me," he pleaded raggedly. His back was moist under Glory's hands, and she could see a fine sheen of perspiration glistening on his forehead and along his upper lip.

Her own body was catching fire, and she was moving faster and faster to meet his thrusts and increase the friction. "Jesse—you know—I do—"

"Say it!"

"I love you," she gasped as her body arched suddenly, like a bowstring drawn taut, and pleasure splintered through her. "Oh, God, Jesse, *I love you!*"

Now, lying on a made-down couch in her mother's living room a full decade later, Glory wept. Those two trusting, innocent children were gone for all eternity, replaced by angry and embittered adults who could barely exchange a civil word.

In the morning, just as she'd expected, Glory looked terrible. Her eyes were puffy and red-rimmed, and there were shadows underneath them, purple as bruises. She showered, put on jeans and a navy blue turtleneck sweater, and pulled her hair back into a French braid. Knowing there would be no hiding the ravages of the night before, she wore very little makeup—just some blusher and lip gloss.

Delphine presented her with a steaming cup of coffee and a bowl of hot oatmeal when she arrived in the bustling diner. The short-order cook was busy in the kitchen, frying up traditional breakfasts for a hungry crowd.

Glory tried to fade into the wall at the end of the counter, but there was no such luck. People knew she was back in town, and they were anxious to talk with her.

No sooner had the telephone lineman gotten off his stool to go out and battle the weather than someone else replaced him. By the time she'd finished her breakfast, Glory had explained to three people that she'd be staying on in Pearl River for a while and agreed just as often that, yes, it was about time her mother finally remarried.

She was just about to make an escape when the little bells over the diner's door jingled and a stream of cold air swept into the warm, brightly lit interior.

"Good heavens, Jesse," Delphine fussed as she set four breakfast specials down in front of as many customers, "shut the door. The furnace in this place burns five-dollar bills!"

Glory felt her throat go tight, as she watched Jesse push the door closed and grin at Delphine. It seemed to Glory that everyone in the place was either looking at him or at her.

"Sorry," he said, taking off his snow-dusted hat with an exaggerated politeness.

At the same time he was zeroing in on the empty stool next to Glory. Reaching it, he turned and looked at her with eyes as cold as the slush outside in the gutter and said, "I brought your car to town."

She would have stood, but he reached out and caught hold of her forearm, effectively pressing her back down.

"Thank you, Jesse," he coached, and though he sounded as though he was teasing, his dark eyes snapped.

"Go to hell," Glory replied in a normal tone. She wasn't about to forget what this man had stolen from her.

Delphine had always said Jesse's grin ought to be registered as a lethal weapon, and he obviously had no compunctions about using it. He smiled at Glory and, for just a moment, she was a teenager again, willing to share her body and soul with this man.

"There's something on the seat of your car that you might be interested in," he said. Then he pushed away from the counter and strolled toward the door, stopping to joke with some of his constituents as he went.

Glory waited until he'd driven away with the waiting Deputy Johnson before hurrying out to her car. She found a plastic bag lying on the seat, filled with snapshots and school photos of Liza. Glory held the package close to her heart as she sped up the outside stairs to the privacy of Delphine's apartment.

While this unexpected gift might have surprised other people, Glory knew it was typical of Jesse. Even when he was angry with someone, he was still more inclined toward kindness than anything else.

She poured coffee in the tiny kitchenette and sat down at her mother's table to go over the pictures, one by one, noting even the smallest changes as

Liza progressed from a plump infant to a shy fourth-grader.

"Don't worry, kid," Glory whispered, smiling through her tears. "You'll get past this gangly stage, I promise. And you'll be the prettiest girl in Pearl River."

After putting the pictures carefully back into their plastic bag, she grabbed her purse and coat and went downstairs once more. The breakfast rush was slowing down, but Delphine and her helper were still pretty busy.

"I'm driving back to Portland today, after I stop by Ilene Bainbridge's bookstore," Glory told her mother.

Delphine looked as though she'd drop the tray of dirty dishes she'd gathered up. "What?"

"I just want to pick up a few things I left in storage, Mama. My resumé, some job-hunting clothes. I'll be back tonight."

"Those roads are icy," Delphine warned. "You be careful, and call when you arrive."

Glory kissed her mother's cheek. "I will. See you."

Five minutes later, Glory's car nosed to a stop in the hard, dry snow in front of Ilene's Book Store. Parallel parking had never caught on in Pearl River; people still left their cars at right angles to the sidewalk, the way they'd left horses and wagons years before.

There were Christmas lights in the window of the bookstore, along with a display of crystals catching the cold winter light.

Glory pushed open the door and walked in.

The place had a friendly ambience; there was a rocking chair, complete with a gray tabby cat curled up on the cushion, and a cheerful fire burned in a small Franklin stove. The selection of books, Glory saw at a glance, was eclectic.

"Hello?" Glory called, when no one appeared to wait on her.

A plump woman dressed in a caftan of gold-and-mauve paisley came out of a back room, smiling. Her brown hair was braided and wound into a coronet at her nape, with a bright yellow feather for accent.

"Jesse's friend, Glory," she said with a smile.

Given the new-age flavor of the place, Glory wondered for a moment if the woman was psychic. "Just Glory," she corrected quietly.

"Ilene Bainbridge," the bookshop owner said, extending a bejeweled hand. "I've been hearing about you for years, and just lately the news has gotten even more interesting. It's good to finally make your acquaintance." She shooed away the tabby cat and gestured for Glory to sit down in the rocking chair. "Would you like a cup of licorice tea?"

Before Glory could respond, Ilene disappeared again. Her voice came clearly from the back room.

"Shall I add sugar?"

Glory was looking out the window, watching as fat snowflakes began tumbling from the sky. "Just a teaspoon, please."

Ilene returned with two steaming cups. Handing one to Glory, she pulled up a plain folding chair and sat down. Her kind eyes were eager and warm. "It's nice to sit by a fire on a day like this," she commented.

Sipping her tea, Glory nodded. "Jesse tells me that Liza spends most of her time here with you."

Since Ilene didn't look at all surprised at the sudden shift in conversation, Glory assumed Jesse had told her about their relationship and her claim that Liza was her child. The other woman, who was probably in her late thirties, smiled. "Liza and I have a little apartment upstairs."

Glory sensed that Ilene was a gentle, even-tempered woman. She was probably very good to Liza. "I take it she's had a difficult life so far," she said, feeling guilty. In those moments, Glory sorely regretted not standing up to Judge Bainbridge and going straight to Jesse with the news of her pregnancy. In trying to protect Dylan, she had caused her daughter a lot of pain and upheaval.

Ilene's smile was gentle. "It's been eventful, that's for certain. But we love Liza, Jesse and I, and she knows it. That goes a long way toward making a child feel secure. Lately, though, she has developed a tendency to speculate almost incessantly about her birth parents."

Glory thought of the house her mother and Harold had bought, and suddenly she wanted with all her heart to live in a place like that with Liza and Jesse. Of course she knew it was impossible—just a Christmas fantasy. She would never trust Jesse again, and he'd never trust her.

"I want Liza to be happy," Glory said, near tears herself.

Ilene reached out and patted her hand. "Jesse told me you were planning to stick around, and I think that's a good idea. You never know what might happen."

Glory set her teacup aside and smiled at the tabby cat, who was curled up a few feet away on the hooked rug in front of the stove, waiting for the human intruder to get out of the rocking chair. "Thank you," she said to Ilene, standing.

The other woman rose and took Glory's teacup. "You'd be welcome to stop by any time," she said. "Even if you weren't shopping for books."

Glory got the message. When she wanted to see Liza, she would be a welcome guest at the bookstore. That was certainly more than she could say for any reception she might get at Jesse's place. "I'll remember," she replied.

She left the store and got back into her car, cranking up the heat and turning on the tape deck. It was a three-hour drive to Portland, and if she wanted to be back before nightfall, she would have to hurry.

Accordingly, five minutes later, Glory was speeding down the open road. The highway had been sanded, and although there were lots of cars in the ditch from the night before, driving conditions were good. The snow had stopped and patches of blue sky were visible in the distance, along with clouds that looked like well-used cotton balls.

She drove straight through, except for a brief stop at the drive-in window of a fast-food restaurant for lunch, and when she reached the storage place, it took a long time to locate the particular boxes she wanted. She found an expensive gold bracelet Alan had given her in the pocket of a tweed blazer.

On impulse she drove to his apartment building, meaning to leave the piece with one of his neighbors, but his car was parked in the lot, so she knocked on the door. Something inside made her want Alan to know she was all right; that she had hopes and plans, that he hadn't destroyed her.

"Come in, it's open!" he called out, and when Glory stepped inside, she saw that he was packing up his books.

Glory felt only a slight ache in her heart at the sight of him. He was a good-looking man, with his dark hair and blue eyes, but she knew she didn't love him. Maybe she never had.

"Hi," she said, closing the door. "I thought you'd be working." She held up the bracelet. "I just wanted to leave this."

Alan nodded, a sad grin lifting one corner of his mouth. "The bank is sending me to work in one of its outlying branches. You can probably appreciate the irony of that."

Glory was taken aback. If what Alan said was true, she could probably return to her old job right there in Portland. She'd been decisive when she gave notice, but not rude.

Just a few days ago, that position had meant everything to her, but now she could hardly wait to be in Pearl River again. "I'm moving back to my hometown," she said. It seemed strange that she'd once thought she loved this man desperately. Now he seemed insipid, even a little on the wimpy side.

Alan paused in the packing of books to rest his hands on his hips. "Ah, yes—Pearl River. The heartbeat of the American financial community."

Glory ignored his sarcasm, drew a deep breath, and took a step backward, reaching for the door knob. "Well, Alan—goodbye, and good luck in your new job."

He stretched out a hand toward her. "Glory, stay. At least have dinner with me—we can part friends."

"We can never be friends," Glory responded, and then she opened the door and went out. The moist, chilly wind felt good on her face.

Alan followed her all the way to her car. "I suppose you arrived in the old hometown and found out none of the local women had managed to sink their claws into Jesse Bainbridge," he said, his arms folded across his chest.

She swallowed. "This has nothing to do with Jesse," she said. It wasn't the complete truth, but none of this was any of Alan's business, anyway. "Besides, I think I'm a small-town girl. The cutthroat ways of big-city banking are not for me."

Alan jammed the fingers of one hand through his hair. "Damn it, Glory, I only wanted that promotion so you and I could finally get married and start a family. I knew that wouldn't happen if you were up to your eyeballs in loan applications and appraisals—"

"You *knew*," Glory corrected, "that I'd studied and slaved for that job for years. And when my back was turned, you elbowed your way in."

"Glory, I'm sorry," he said.

She opened the car door. "Gee," she replied cuttingly, batting her eyelashes at him. "You're *sorry*. Well, why didn't you say so before, Alan? That just changes everything."

With that, she got behind the wheel and slammed the door.

Alan slammed his hands down on the hood of her car in pure frustration, and although Glory had never known him to be violent before, she was angered and frightened by the action. She shoved the engine into reverse and sped away.

Reaching the edge of the city, she stopped at a busy restaurant for a cup of coffee and a sandwich. While she was waiting for her order, she went to the pay phone and dialed Delphine's number at the diner.

"Hello, Mama," she said, when her mother answered. "I arrived safely, and now I'm ready to leave again. I'll see you in a few hours."

Delphine's quicksilver sense of humor came through just at the moment when Glory needed it most. "Who is this?" she asked.

4

Glory arrived back in Pearl River, as promised, before nightfall. She and Delphine and Harold had dinner out in nearby Fawn Creek and went Christmas shopping at the mall, another new addition since Glory had first left home.

The next morning she put on a suede suit in a pale shade of rose, accented with a cream-colored silk blouse and gold jewelry, and went down the street to the bank to pay a call on Harvey Baker. Glory hadn't forgotten her mother's remarking, that first day, that Mr. Baker needed an assistant, since the old one had taken a job in Seattle.

Mr. Baker was a substantial man with a full head of white hair and exceptional manners. And he'd already heard that Glory was looking for a job. He took her into his modest office, looked over the resumé she presented, and hired her on the spot.

Glory left the bank feeling almost euphoric. Now all she needed was a place of her own, so she could get out of her mother's way. She called the town's only motel, but it was full. Then she telephoned the real-estate agency and learned there was a one-bedroom place available in an old Victorian house down by the river.

By the time she went into the diner for a very late lunch, Glory not only had a job but a place to live. She would make arrangements for her furniture and personal belongings to be moved as soon as possible.

"Don't you think you're being a little hasty, here?" Delphine asked, when they were alone in the diner after the lunch rush. The fry cook was outside in the alley, arguing with the man who delivered fresh produce. "Glory, maybe it would be better if you just went on with your life and tried to forget about Liza."

"Forget her?" Glory's spoon rattled in her coffee cup as she stirred unnecessarily. The two women were sitting at a table close to the counter. "Mama, could you have ever forgotten Dylan and me?"

"Of course not, but it wasn't the same. I didn't just give birth to you, I raised you." For a moment she averted her eyes, displaying great interest in the rusted metal thermometer affixed to the outside window casing. The snow was coating it, hiding its imperfections. Finally Delphine looked back at her daughter again. "Glory, Jesse's involved with somebody. Her name's Adara Simms and she owns the beauty shop.''

Although she wouldn't have shown it, the reminder made Glory feel as though she'd just been slammed in the stomach with a board. She *had* been fostering a fantasy that included Jesse and Liza, whether she wanted to or not, neatly ignoring Adara's existence, and she realized now what dangerous emotional ground she'd been on. ''Why didn't you tell me this the other night,'' she asked moderately, ''when you were so sure I had a date with Jesse?''

Delphine sighed. ''That was before Mavis Springbeiger came in and told me Jesse planned to give Adara an engagement ring for Christmas.''

Glory closed her eyes tightly for a moment. Lord, but it hurt, the idea of Jesse slipping a ring onto someone else's finger. She didn't dare imagine the wedding itself. ''I see,'' she said woodenly.

Her mother reached out and closed her hand over Glory's fingers, to still their trembling with a squeeze. ''Honey, you're young, you're beautiful—you're smart and educated. You don't need Jesse, or even Liza, to make your life complete. There are other men to love you, and you can still have all the babies you want. *Please,* don't limit yourself by staying here and living for the occasional glimpse of your daughter!''

Glory understood what her mother was saying, and it all made sense to her intellect. But her heart, never very amenable to logic, was balking. She sniffled. "If I didn't know better, Mama, I'd swear you were trying to get rid of me."

There were tears in Delphine's eyes, even though she was smiling. "Heaven help me, Glory Parsons, if my conscience would allow it I'd beg you to stay. But I love you very much, and I want you to have the best possible life."

The bell tinkled over the door, and long habit made Delphine stand up and smooth her crisp apron. When she saw that the visitor was Jesse, however, she didn't offer any of her standard greetings. She tossed her daughter a meaningful look and disappeared into the kitchen.

Without being invited, Jesse dragged back Delphine's chair and sat. The expression in his caramel eyes was guarded, and there was a stubborn set to his jaw. Glory sensed that he was full of questions, that beneath his calm exterior was an urge to grab her and shake her until she told him everything about her past.

"You sure know how to clear a room," Glory said, because somebody had to say something and it was clear Jesse wasn't going to extend the courtesy first.

He managed a rigid smile, and Glory noticed that there were snowflakes melting in his glossy brown hair. Jesse had never liked hats. "Ilene told me you visited her yesterday."

Glory drew a deep breath and let it out slowly. "Guilty," she confessed, raising one hand as if to give an oath.

He sat back in his chair for a long moment, regarding Glory as though he expected her to do or say something outlandish. Then he muttered, "I'm prepared to concede that Liza is our child."

"That's big of you," Glory replied smoothly, getting up from her chair and going behind the counter for a cup and a pot of coffee. She poured a cupful for Jesse, refilled her own, and returned the pot to its place before going on. "I assumed you'd come to terms with the idea, when you gave me those pictures of Liza. Thank you for that, by the way."

Now Jesse leaned forward, ignoring the steaming coffee before him. "What I'm *not* willing to concede," he went on, as though she hadn't spoken, "is that you have any right to interfere with Liza's life now. She's been through enough, as it is. I don't want her upset."

Glory's hands trembled as she lifted her cup to her mouth and took a sip. Delphine's coffee was legendary, since she added a secret ingredient before brewing it, but the stuff passed over Glory's tongue untasted. "I've never said I would tell Liza who I am," she said evenly, once she'd swallowed. "I just want to spend time with her. And I will, Jesse, whether you like it or not."

Again, Jesse's jawline tightened. He took a packet of sugar from the container and turned it end over end on the tabletop. "You gave her up," he said. "You handed her over to the authorities and walked away. As far as I'm concerned you made your decision then, and you can't go back on it now."

Glory's instincts warned her to drop the subject for the moment. Jesse wasn't feeling real receptive just then, and pushing would only make him more stubborn. "I hear you're getting married." She said the words as cheerfully as she could.

He averted his wonderful brown eyes, gazing out at the drifting snow, and for a moment he looked so desolate that Glory wanted to put her arms around him and offer him whatever comfort she could. "You hear a lot of things in small towns," he murmured. Then he pushed back his chair and stood. "You're not going to give ground on this, are you? You're going to insist on hanging around."

Glory felt color pool in her cheeks, and she knew her eyes were shooting blue sparks. She'd tried to be civil, but Jesse evidently wasn't going to allow that. "Yes, Jesse," she said quietly. "I'll be staying in Pearl River. I have a job and an apartment."

"Great," he rasped, shoving a hand through his snow-dampened hair.

"There's an old adage, Jesse, about accepting the things you can't change. This is one of those things."

He bit out a curse word. "I suppose you're planning to drag some big-city lawyer into this."

Glory straightened her shoulders. She was glad she was still wearing her suede suit, because it gave her an added air of dignity. "If necessary, I will. But it doesn't have to be that way."

Jesse turned and walked away without another word. The little bell over the door jangled angrily as he wrenched open the door and left.

Delphine came out of the kitchen. "I have to hand it to you, Glory—you were diplomatic."

"I tried," Glory answered. She wanted to go upstairs, throw herself down on the sofa and sob, but she couldn't face the emotional hangover that would come afterward. She glanced at the clock on the wall behind the counter and sighed. "Do you need any help?"

"Roxy will be coming in at the regular time," Delphine replied sympathetically. "You've had a big day. Why don't you get some lunch and then go upstairs and take a nice nap?''

Glory chuckled, but there wasn't even a hint of humor in the sound. ''Mama, it's only eleven-thirty in the morning. Do I look like such a wreck that I should be in bed convalescing?''

''Yes,'' Delphine retorted. But she was smiling.

''Well, I'm not going to lie around with a rose in my teeth,'' her daughter said firmly. ''I have things to do. The first of which is to call the moving company and ask them to bring my furniture. Then I'd better do a little emergency shopping. I'm going to need some stuff to tide me over, in the meantime.''

Delphine's expressive eyes went wide. ''Nonsense. You can just stay with me until your things arrive. I don't want you camping out in some apartment, sleeping on the floor and eating your meals out of aluminum trays.''

Glory took her coat from a hook by the door and put it on. Slinging her purse strap over her shoulder, she smiled and replied, ''Mama, I called the Stay Awhile Motel, but there's no room at the inn. You're madly in love and about to be married. What you don't need right now is a woebegone daughter sleeping on your sofa.''

With that, Glory went out into the biting wind again and up the stairs to her mother's apartment. After making the necessary arrangements for her belongings to be brought to Pearl River, she came back downstairs and climbed behind the wheel of her car. Praying her snow tires were as good as the people in the TV commercials maintained, she set out for the mall in the next town.

There, she bought a sleeping bag and an air mattress, a card table and two cheap folding chairs, towels and other necessary household items. Then she returned to Pearl River, driving cautiously in the ever-wilder flurries of snow to the supermarket at the north end of town.

She couldn't help noticing that people were pointing to her and whispering. Glory was sure none of them knew about the baby she'd borne nine years before, but there was no question that the inevitable small-town speculation was going on. The general population was obviously wondering why she'd left town so suddenly all those years before, deserting "poor Jesse Bainbridge" without so much as a fare-thee-well, and whether or not she'd prove to be a problem where his new relationship was concerned.

After she'd taken everything to her empty, chilly apartment and put it away, Glory went on impulse to Ilene's bookstore. Heaven knew, the woman was nothing if not unconventional, but there was a quiet warmth about her that drew the troubled spirit.

Glory had no doubt that the local bookseller was a trusted confidante to many people.

Ilene was busy with a customer when Glory entered, but she still greeted her with a wide and welcoming smile and a "come-in" gesture of one beringed hand.

Glory went to the shelves and busied herself selecting mystery novels. She had a passion for the books, especially if they boasted some unusual element, such as a vampire or a werewolf.

"I take it you've talked to Jesse recently," Ilene said softly, startling her newest customer. Glory hadn't heard her approach.

"You must be psychic," Glory replied with a sigh.

Ilene smiled and glanced at the books in Glory's hands. "You don't have to buy things for an excuse to talk to me," she said. "I consider you a friend, and you're welcome here any time."

Glory felt quick, illogical tears burn behind her eyes, but she managed to hold them back. She held the books a little tighter. "I read a lot," she said in a small voice.

Ilene took her arm and gently ushered her toward the rocker and the warm stove. She shooed away the tabby cat and bid her guest to sit down. "What did Jesse say to you?" she asked, taking the other chair.

After a pause, Glory replied with a despondent shrug, and said, "He thinks I ought to leave town." Although neither woman had ever mentioned the fact, Glory knew Ilene was aware Glory had borne Jesse's child, and that the child was Liza.

Ilene sat forward in her chair, her hands calmly folded. "Will you?"

Glory shook her head, arranging and rearranging the paperback books on her lap. "No. I must admit my mother suggested the same thing—that I just go on with my life somewhere else—but I can't. Something inside insists on staying right here where I can be close to my child."

"Then that's probably what you should do," Ilene commented. "Do you plan to tell Liza who you are?"

"No," Glory replied quickly. "That would only confuse her. I just want to be her friend, and I don't know why Jesse can't understand that."

Ilene smiled. "He's not trying, at least not at the moment. But I'm sure this has all been a terrific shock to him. After all, it isn't every day a man finds out that his niece is really his daughter. Jesse must feel as though he's wandered onto the set of a soap opera."

"I know," Glory agreed with a nod. "Believe me, I didn't expect to come home for Christmas and my mother's wedding and find out that the baby I'd given away was right here in Pearl River, being raised as a part of the Bainbridge family."

With a chuckle and a responding nod, Ilene got up to brew tea. She returned minutes later with two steaming cups.

"This time it's chamomile," she said. "That's really soothing, you know."

Glory was all for anything that would calm her jangling nerves.

"I'll talk to Jesse myself," Ilene said decisively, while her guest sipped herbal tea. "Perhaps I can get him to see reason."

"I'd be very grateful," Glory said. "I don't really want to approach Liza until Jesse gives me some kind of go-ahead, but I can't wait forever."

"Of course you can't," Ilene agreed as an older man bustled eagerly in from the cold.

Glory recognized him as Mr. Pellis, the principal at Pearl River High back when she and Jesse were in school.

"Got any more of that tea, Ilene?" he demanded jovially, in that booming voice that had called a halt to so many food fights and hallway spit-wad barrages. "This weather is enough to chill a man to the marrow!"

Ilene bustled back to brew another cupful, and Mr. Pellis turned his kindly gaze to Glory.

"Aren't you the Parsons girl?" he asked. "The one who took up two pages in your class's senior yearbook?"

Glory smiled, nodded, and started to stand, but Mr. Pellis gestured for her to remain seated. He took off his hat, revealing a perfectly bald head, and then his scarf and overcoat, and hung all the items up.

"I'm retired now," Mr. Pellis went on, taking Ilene's chair. He tapped his temple with one finger. "But I remember things. You dated the Bainbridge boy, didn't you?"

Glory swallowed and nodded again. She supposed she shouldn't be surprised that Jesse found his way into virtually every conversation. After all, this was Pearl River, his hometown, and he was sheriff.

Mr. Pellis chuckled and slapped his thighs with both hands. "Always thought you'd end up in the movies or something, you were so pretty. What do you do for a living?"

"I'm a loan officer," Glory replied, rising from her chair. It was getting late, and Delphine would be watching for her. "As of Monday morning, I'll be working right down the street at the First National."

Mr. Pellis beamed as though she'd just been elected president and he was personally responsible. "Well, good," he said. "I'll stop by and say hello when I drop off my pension check."

Glory's smile was warm. "I'll be expecting you," she said. Then she paid Ilene for her books and went back to the diner.

She was curled up on the couch, dressed in jeans, sneakers and a red turtleneck sweater, reading one of the mysteries she'd bought, when the telephone jangled.

Startled, Glory jumped before reaching out to snatch up the receiver. "Hello?" she said a little uncharitably.

"Hello," responded a voice she immediately recognized. "This is Jesse." He sounded weary and more than a little annoyed, and Glory guessed without being told that Ilene had talked with him. She held her breath, waiting for him to go on.

After a long, electric silence, he did.

"They still have that community Christmas Party every year, with the sleigh riding and everything," he announced, each word dragged out of him by an invisible mule team. "It's tomorrow night, and I was wondering if you'd like to go. I mean, it won't be a date or anything, because Adara will be along, but you've been wanting to spend time with Liza...."

Glory was well aware that, as a beggar, she couldn't be a chooser. "Thanks," she said softly. Sincerely. "I appreciate it."

"I don't want you telling her anything."

Who, Glory wanted to ask, *Liza or Adara?* But she controlled herself because she was in no position to be making smart remarks. "I've already told you, Jesse—I won't say anything to Liza that would upset her. You can trust me."

"I thought I could, once," he responded in a distracted voice, and Glory closed her eyes against the pain of the jibe. "Listen, just meet us at the hill tomorrow night when the sun goes down. We'll be somewhere around the bonfire."

Glory was nodding, and it was a moment before she realized Jesse couldn't see her and said quickly, "I'll be there. Thanks, Jesse."

"Right," he answered in the clipped tone she'd come to expect from him. And then he hung up.

Glory bounded off the couch, upsetting her book and the crocheted afghan she'd spread over herself earlier. "Yippee!" she yelled.

The cry brought Delphine out of the bedroom, where she'd been dressing for a bowling date with Harold. "You won the lottery?" she inquired with a wry grin.

"Better," Glory crowed. "Jesse's going to let me see Liza."

Although Delphine shook her head, her eyes revealed a mother's happiness in her daughter's joy. She came and took both Glory's hands in hers. "Promise me you'll be careful, baby," she whispered. "This situation has a very high heartache potential—especially for you."

Glory was deflated for a moment, but she immediately perked up. "Jesse did make a point of telling me he was bringing Adara, but I'm not going to let that ruin things. He can marry King Kong, for all I care, just as long as I get to see Liza."

Delphine patted her daughter's cheeks. "Like I said, be careful. Here be dragons, fair maiden. Big ones, with fire in their noses."

Glory chuckled and kissed Delphine's forehead. "I'll get through this without so much as a singed eyelash," she promised.

But Delphine didn't look convinced.

Glory spent the night at her new apartment, staying up late to finish the first of the mystery novels she'd bought because she was too excited to sleep. The place was freezing cold when she awakened, and she shivered while trying to crank on the ancient steam radiators that stood under each window.

Outside, the world was a wonderland of white velvet strewn with tiny diamonds. Snow mounded on top of the row of mailboxes across the street and the cars parked on the road.

After taking a shower and dressing warmly, with long underwear under her jeans and flannel shirt and two pairs of socks inside her hiking boots, Glory donned a jacket and walked to the diner. Her breath made white plumes in the air, and the cold turned her cheeks and nose red.

By the time she reached her destination, she figured she probably looked a lot like Rudolph.

Delphine greeted her as though she'd spent the night in an igloo in the Arctic, shuffling her to a table, pouring coffee for her, insisting that she have a hot breakfast.

"You're not used to this, after Portland's milder climate," Delphine fretted.

Glory just smiled. She'd been on her own a long time, and Alan had never been much for making a fuss. It was sort of nice to have somebody taking care of her, at least for a few minutes.

After breakfast, Glory insisted on staying to help with dishes and then the noon rush. She was living for that evening when she would see Liza, and if she didn't keep busy in the meantime she'd go absolutely crazy.

Once the lunch clientele had eaten and gone, however, things slowed down considerably. Glory called Jill, and the two of them went to a matinee at the Rialto.

"I've always said Ted Danson was wasted as a bartender," Jill commented as she and Glory left the theater about two hours later.

Glory chuckled. "Are you going to the snow party tonight?" she asked.

Jill shook her head. "Normally I would. But I've got a hot date with a guy over in Fawn Creek. Wish me luck." They crossed the street to where Jill's car was parked—behind a four-foot pile of snow. "The mad plower has struck again."

A teenage boy came out of the hardware store wearing a heavy coat and blushing, either from the cold or from the presence of two women, to shovel a path for Jill. Soon Glory's friend was driving away, tooting her horn and waving.

Glory looked at her watch and groaned. It was still hours until time for the community party.

Finally, however, the time came. She rode to McCalley's Hill, which overlooked the town, with Harold and Delphine, who were bundled up and equipped with hot cocoa in a big thermos bottle. An enormous bonfire was blazing in the big clearing at the bottom of the slope, and already kids and adults alike were racing down the long incline on their sleds.

When Glory spotted Jesse standing with Liza and a slender woman dressed in a pink quilted ski outfit, she was struck by a sudden attack of shyness. Now that the moment she'd been looking forward to for twenty-four hours had finally come, she wasn't sure how to approach the trio, and she had no idea what to say.

Delphine solved the problem by gripping Glory by one arm and fairly propelling her into the cozy little circle. "Hello, Jesse," Glory's mother said with a bright smile. "Liza, Adara, I'd like you to meet my daughter, Glory."

Adara had dark hair and beautiful brown eyes, Glory noticed, but her attention immediately shifted to Liza.

The child looked up at her with an unhesitating, friendly smile. "Hi," she said. "I've seen you in Uncle Jesse's yearbook. It says, 'Glory, Glory, Hallelujah' over your picture."

Adara's gaze came quickly to Glory's face, and there was something sad in it.

"It's just a play on my name," Glory told Liza. "Listen, I'm new in town..." She carefully avoided Jesse's gaze, though she could feel it burning against her face, just like the bonfire. "Well, okay, I'm not new, but I've been away for a long time, and I could use a friend to go sledding with."

Liza, who was apparently a naturally gregarious child, looked delighted and pointed to her nifty Red Flier. "I'll share with you. Come on!"

Glory was intent on following Liza up the hill, when Jesse reached out and took a tight hold on her arm.

"Remember," he said cryptically.

Glory understood him all too well. "Your orders are burned into my gray cells, Sheriff Bainbridge," she replied with a cocky grin and a salute, and then she hurried after the eager little girl pulling a sled behind her.

She and Liza raced down the hill on the sled among a horde of other sledders, and then, laughing, ran up again. They repeated the process until their cheeks, feet and mittened hands were numb.

"I think we'd better stand by the fire for a while and have something warm to drink, don't you?" Glory suggested breathlessly to the sturdy child standing beside her, surveying the hillside with an attitude of conquest.

Liza sighed, her green eyes rising to Glory's face. She smiled, and her freckles showed like specks of gold in the firelight. "Okay," she said. Her gaze was full of generous curiosity. "You said you were new in town. Where do you live? Do you have a job?"

Glory explained about her new position at the bank and her apartment in the blue-and-gray Victorian house near the bend in the river.

Liza was familiar with both places.

Adara was standing next to the fire, sipping cider, when Glory and Liza approached with cups of their own. There was no sign of Jesse, and his girlfriend looked politely uncomfortable.

While Liza was occupied talking to a friend a few feet away, Adara smiled shakily and asked, "Will you be staying in Pearl River long?"

Glory sensed the woman's fears and felt a strange need to reassure her. "Yes, as a matter of fact, I plan to settle here. I'll be working at the bank."

Adara seemed composed, although her hand trembled a little, causing some of her cider to spill over into the snow. "Isn't that nice," she said, and though she didn't speak unkindly, there was no conviction in the words.

Before Glory could reply, Adara spotted some people she knew, trilled out a hello, and hurried off toward them.

Glory was relieved. Adara was probably a relatively new arrival in Pearl River, but she had to know that Jesse and Glory had been high-school sweethearts. Like every small town, this little burg had its busybody contingent.

"Ready to go again?" Liza asked eagerly, just as Glory was finishing her cider.

"Sure!" Glory responded. She was exhausted and cold, but she would have sledded forever if it meant she could be close to her daughter. She would be grateful until the day she died for the child's ready acceptance.

Each of them took hold of the rope and pulled the Flier up the hill, careful to stay out of the way of the sleds zooming down from the top. Once they reached the summit, however, Jesse appeared out of nowhere.

The look he gave Glory was one of annoyance, as though he'd been dragged to the crest of that hill, kicking and screaming. "Once for old time's sake?" he asked, and the words were, of course, unwillingly spoken.

Glory remembered the winters she and Jesse had sledded down this very slope together, and her heart rate quickened by a beat or two. She looked at Liza and tried to speak in a normal tone of voice. "Would that be okay with you?"

Liza looked pleased, and the pom-pom on the top of her blue stocking cap bobbed as she nodded her head.

Glory settled on the front of the sled, instead of the back as she would have with Liza, and shivered a little when she felt the warmth of Jesse's breath against her nape. He wrapped his legs around her and hooked his heels into the front of the sled, then his arms embraced her, his hands gripping the rope.

They went careening down the hillside, the wind rushing in their faces, cold enough to sting. At the bottom the sled suddenly overturned and sent them both tumbling over the snow.

When they finally came to a stop, Jesse was lying on top of Glory. He swore and rolled away, but not before she felt the hard evidence of his desire pressing against her thigh.

5

Jesse dropped Liza off at Ilene's first, then drove to Adara's condo overlooking the river.

She stood waiting for his kiss there on her doorstep, and for the life of him Jesse couldn't give it.

"You might as well tell me about Glory," she said quietly, holding her chin at a proud angle. "I run a beauty shop, remember, and by Monday afternoon I'll know every sordid detail."

He jammed splayed fingers through his hair and swallowed a curse. "We went together in high school, all right?" he finally bit out a few seconds later.

Adara pretended to recoil slightly. "Aren't we defensive?" she inquired sweetly. "I'm not a fool, Jesse. I've already guessed that you loved her."

Loved her? He'd been so crazy about Glory that he couldn't put one sensible thought in front of another. And after she'd left without one damn word of explanation, he'd honestly thought he was going to die of the pain. He'd hounded her family and friends for weeks, trying to find out where she'd gone.

"What do kids that age know about love?" he countered irritably.

"Sometimes a lot," Adara replied.

"I don't want to talk about it."

"That's obvious, Jesse. But I can't let things go at that. I won't stumble along, thinking you and I have a future together, only to find out that you're still hung up on your high-school sweetheart."

Jesse thought of the diamond engagement ring he'd bought. Until just a few days ago, he'd been sure he'd finally reached the point where he could put Glory out of his mind, get married and start the family he wanted more than anything else. Now he felt as though he'd just collided with a linebacker at a dead run; not only did he hurt everywhere, he no longer knew down from up, or in from out.

"Jesse?" Adara prompted.

He hated himself for the heartache he saw in her eyes. She was a nice person, and she didn't deserve to be hurt. "Maybe we'd better cool it for a little while," he said with extreme effort. "Just until the holidays are over and I can think things through."

Adara kissed his cheek, and her hand shook as she turned the key in the lock. So did her voice. "Call me when you've worked it out," she said. And then she opened the door and went inside.

Jesse stifled a roar of outraged frustration and flung himself down the sidewalk toward his truck, which was parked at the curb and still running.

He guessed that said a lot, right there. He hadn't even bothered to shut the engine off, when even a few days before, he would have stayed until just before the sun came up.

Reaching the truck, Jesse jerked off his gloves and flung them into the cab, one after the other, not giving a damn where they landed. Then he got behind the wheel and sped away.

At home, he brought the truck to a lurching stop in the driveway and stormed toward the front door.

Not only had he wounded Adara, he'd stirred up a whole lot of old sensations he didn't want to deal with. Ever since he and Glory had gone flying off that sled—hell, ever since he'd gotten *on* the damn thing with her—he'd ached in every muscle between his eyebrows and his shins.

He opened the door, went inside and slammed it again. Instead of hanging up his bulky coat, he hurled it in the general direction of the coat tree. Then he marched into the living room, to the liquor cabinet, and poured himself a double shot of brandy.

A few sips settled him down a little, and he ventured into his grandfather's study and squinted at the shelves until he found the Pearl River year-book from when he and Glory were seniors.

After tossing back a little more brandy, he carried the annual to the heavy rolltop desk, with all its cubbyholes and drawers, and sat down in the swivel chair. His fingers flipped the pages unerringly to the layout honoring Glory.

She'd been homecoming queen that year, and head cheerleader, and there were shots of her wearing a sun top and cutoff jeans at the senior picnic, making a speech on graduation day, sitting on Santa's lap at the Christmas dance.

Jesse couldn't help smiling at the banner head-line spread across the top of the adjoining pages. *Glory, Glory, Hallelujah.*

"Amen," Jesse said aloud, his gaze going back to the snapshot of Glory at the class picnic. He'd taken her to his room that sultry afternoon and made slow, hot love to her, and she'd responded without holding anything back.

Just the memory made him harden painfully. He slammed the yearbook closed and tossed it onto the desk.

Whatever he did, he had to remember that Glory was Glory. She'd proven beyond a doubt that she cared only about her own interests and she'd betray people who trusted her, to attain her objectives. As delectable as she looked, all grown-up, it was unlikely that she'd changed in any fundamental way.

She wanted Liza, and that meant he had to be on his guard. Despite Glory's protests that she wasn't going to upset the child, Jesse had no illusions about her conscience.

She probably didn't have one.

Still he needed to see her, talk to her, hold her. He phoned the office to let them know he'd be on the road, put his coat back on, and went out to his truck again.

He knew Glory had taken an apartment, he even knew where it was. But some instinct took him by the diner instead, and he saw her through the snow-trimmed window, sitting there all alone, her head bent over a book or something.

Almost as furious with himself as he was with Glory, he parked the truck and strode over to the door.

The "closed" sign was in place and the door was locked, but Glory came and admitted him right away. Her blue eyes were wide and wary, and standing there, Jesse forgot everything he'd meant to say.

"What have I done now?" Glory asked with a sad smile as she relocked the door and went back to the table where she'd been sitting, going over Delphine's quarterly taxes. Earlier, it had seemed like a good, practical way to pass what remained of the evening, as well as an excuse to get out of her lonely apartment.

Jesse helped himself to coffee behind the counter, then crossed the room to join her. After taking off his jacket and hanging it over the back of his chair, he sat down. "I just wanted to tell you that Liza had a really good time with you tonight."

Glory could tell he hadn't meant to say that, and the bewildered expression in his eyes made her feel strangely jubilant. "She's a wonderful, outgoing child," she replied. "You and Ilene must be doing a very good job with her."

He relaxed at that, and took a sip of his coffee. "Ilene strikes most people as a little weird, at first, but she'd walk through fire for Liza, and the kid knows it. That makes for a lot of security."

It was so nice to be talking civilly with Jesse for once that Glory felt her throat tighten. "We had that, Dylan and I, whatever else we were lacking. We both knew Mama was committed to us with her whole heart."

Jesse shifted in his chair, looking slightly uncomfortable again. "I don't remember my parents very well. Gresh was a lot older than I was, of course, and Gramps had his own fish to fry. As you know, he and I never got along very well."

Glory found it impossible to picture that vicious old man in such a homey context as "Gramps." "I've heard your grandfather suffered a couple of strokes and had to be confined to a nursing home. I'm sorry." And she was, though she felt no remorse for hating Seth Bainbridge for so long, just a certain weariness.

"They take good care of him at the convalescent center," Jesse said. He was avoiding her eyes.

Glory glanced down at her mother's receipts and tax forms, at a temporary loss for something to say, and Jesse's chair legs scraped against the linoleum floor as he stood.

The idea of his leaving alarmed Glory, and she was further upset to find herself wanting him to stay.

But he only went to the jukebox and leaned against it, studying the selections. Delphine believed in moldy oldies, as she called them, and many of the songs dated from the fifties and sixties. The latest offerings were from the early seventies.

After a few moments Glory heard a coin drop into the slot, and she braced herself. Sure enough, Jesse chose the ballad that had been playing on the radio when they'd made love for the first time up at the lake.

She squeezed her eyes shut as an avalanche of emotional pain cascaded down on her.

Then Jesse took her hand, pulled her to her feet and into his arms and they danced. Glory was overwhelmed not only by memories but by the presence and the substance and the scent of Jesse. She wanted to melt against him, become a part of him.

He held her close, and the contact was so excruciatingly sweet that it brought tears to Glory's eyes.

"Don't do this," she pleaded in a bare whisper, certain that he understood his power over her and meant to use it. "Please."

He curved a finger under her chin and lifted. The words he said then were the first gentle ones he'd spared her since her return to Pearl River. "All I want is to hold you, Glory."

It wasn't all he wanted, and Glory knew it. She'd felt his need earlier, when they'd fallen off the sled, and she could feel it now. She fought to reason with him, and with herself. "This isn't right. You're engaged."

He maneuvered them over to the switch beside the door and turned off the lights, so that nothing illuminated the diner except for the multicolored glow of the jukebox. Their song finished and started again, and Jesse bent his head to nuzzle at Glory's neck.

"I'm not engaged," he finally countered, his voice a sleepy rumble, his breath making Glory's flesh tingle under its warmth. "I haven't asked Adara to marry me, and I told her tonight that I needed some time."

Glory swallowed and wondered if he felt the tremor of elation that went through her at this announcement. She was quick to remind herself, however, that it didn't really mean anything. For all that he was holding her so tenderly now, a part of Jesse hated her and he wouldn't hesitate to wreak any kind of vengeance he could manage.

"Jesse, go home," she said thickly. "You shouldn't be here."

He spread his hands over her trim bottom and pressed her close against him and, God help her, she couldn't even take a step back in the interest of self-preservation. Her nipples were throbbing beneath her flannel shirt and winter underwear, and there was a soft, expansive ache where Jesse would enter her.

He found her lips with his own and kissed her treacherously, encircling her mouth with the tip of his tongue and then invading her with it. Instead of fighting, she bid him welcome with her own, sliding her arms up his chest and plunging her fingers into his hair.

The kiss ended, but Jesse didn't withdraw. He bit Glory's lower lip lightly and lifted one of his hands to her breast, cupping it in his fingers, teasing the nipple with his thumb.

"Come home with me," he pleaded in a ragged whisper, "or God help me, I'm going to take you right here."

The words brought Glory abruptly to her senses, and she pushed back out of his arms, gasping for breath as though she'd just surfaced after long minutes underwater. "Damn you, Jesse," she sputtered, "we're not eighteen anymore. And you're not going to get back at me for my supposed wrongs by dragging me off to your bed!"

He hooked his fingers in the waistband of her jeans and hauled her forward, so that she collided with his thighs and the hard heat of his shaft. "Remember how it felt when I was lying on top of you in the snow tonight?" he breathed, and Glory was awash in yearning. "I'm surprised we didn't turn the whole hill to slush."

Jesse was right; there was something hot burning between them, even after all that time and heartbreak. He could take her there in the dark diner if he chose to, and she despised him for that power.

"Get out," she ordered with the very last of her strength.

Miraculously he retreated a step, allowing her to put things somewhat back into perspective again. "I want to take you to dinner Monday night," he said. "We need to talk."

Glory still couldn't manage to speak normally. "J-just about Liza," she stammered. "N-no more dancing."

He reached out and touched the tip of her nose in a gesture that was achingly familiar. "No promises," he said hoarsely. And then he opened the door and went out, just as their song began to play for the third time on the jukebox.

Glory spent Sunday working at the diner and then helping Delphine and Harold put away early wedding presents and various personal belongings in their brand new house. The next day she started her job at the bank.

She had a small office and plenty of people wanted to borrow money, since Pearl River seemed to be in some kind of development boom, so the morning went by rapidly. She had lunch in the coffee room with some of the tellers and secretaries, then returned to the pile of work left behind by Mr. Baker's previous assistant.

It was a surprise when, at quarter after three, Glory's office door squeaked open and Liza's bright green eyes peered at her around the edge.

"Am I bothering you?"

Glory couldn't think of anyone she'd rather have seen, though her mind *had* been straying to Jesse with disturbing frequency. Thanks to him, she'd been in misery most of the weekend.

"Of course you're not bothering me," she said quickly. "Come in."

Liza took in the office in a series of thorough glances. "Nice place," she said.

Glory gestured toward a chair. "Sit down, if you'd like."

The child wriggled into the seat facing Glory's desk, unbuttoning her coat at the same time. Although she was the spitting image of Glory's great-grandmother, there were things about Liza that reminded her of Jesse, too, and of herself.

The steady gaze was Jesse's, the tremulous voice her own.

"I'm adopted," Liza announced without preamble.

Glory was grateful for the chair that supported her, because she knew her legs wouldn't have managed it at the moment. "I see," she finally replied after a long time. She remembered then that Ilene had told her Liza thought a lot about her birth parents.

"Susie Harbrecker says my mom and dad didn't want me, so they gave me away."

A momentary desire to find Susie Harbrecker and shake her until her teeth rattled possessed Glory, then she regained her equilibrium. "I'm sure that isn't true," she said as evenly as she could. "There are lots and lots of good reasons why people put babies up for adoption, Liza. Sometimes they're too poor to care for them properly, and sometimes they're too young and immature." *And scared,* Glory added in her mind.

Liza gave a philosophical sigh, apparently willing to accept Glory's words at face value. She seemed naturally drawn to Glory, just as Glory was to her. "I'm going to be in the Christmas program at church."

Glory smiled, relaxing a bit. "I know. I watched you practice one night."

That seemed to please Liza, but then she frowned. "Of course, I'll probably have trouble coming up with an angel costume. Aunt Ilene sewed in one of her past lives, but she doesn't know how anymore."

Before Glory could comment on that startling statement, there was a brisk rap at the door and then Jesse came in. His expression was stormy, as though he'd just caught Glory plotting the downfall of the free-enterprise system.

If Liza picked up any of the difficult undercurrents in the room, she gave no sign of it. "Hi, Uncle Jesse," she chirped, jumping up and throwing her arms around him.

He gave her an easy hug, but his dark eyes were fixed on Glory, and they were full of wariness and suspicion. "Why don't you wait outside in the car?" he asked politely, his hand resting on Liza's shoulder. "I want to talk with Ms. Parsons for a moment."

Somewhat reluctantly, Liza said goodbye to Glory and left.

"That was some pretty fancy detective work," Glory said, when they were alone. "How did you know she was here?"

He braced his hands against the edge of her desk and leaned forward, glowering ominously into her face. "I know everything that goes on in this town, so don't try to pull anything."

Glory snapped the pencil she was holding into two pieces, though her manner was otherwise pleasant. Or at least courteous. "Why are you acting like I was about to kidnap her and head for South America? We were only talking."

"You have a nasty habit of skipping out at the most inopportune moments," Jesse said. "I wouldn't put anything past you."

"Then there would seem to be no point in our going out to dinner tonight and talking this thing over like adults. You've already drawn the battle lines."

Jesse sighed raggedly and turned away to stand at the office's one window. Once again, snow was coming down. "Maybe I did overreact," he conceded in a barely audible voice. He looked back at her over one sturdy shoulder. "I don't know if I can talk this out with you, Glory, when I haven't even managed to work it through for myself yet."

"Have you told Liza that you're her father?"

He rested his back against the sill and folded his arms. "No," he replied. "She's a sharp kid. If I told her, it wouldn't be long before she guessed who her mother is."

"What would be so terrible about that?"

Jesse thrust himself away from the window, crossed the small room, and opened the door. "It would give you a kind of power I don't want you to have," he answered flatly. "I'll pick you up at six and we'll have dinner in Fawn Creek, if that's all right with you. They've got a pretty classy Mexican place."

Glory couldn't imagine why she wasn't refusing to go out with him, why she wasn't telling Jesse Bainbridge what to do with his Mexican dinner. "Okay," she said. "You know where I live?"

He raised one eyebrow. "I know where you live," he responded. And then, to Glory's enormous relief, he was gone.

At five she left the office, bundled up in her coat, laughing and talking with the other employees who were on their way out, too. In just a few minutes she arrived at her apartment.

There, Glory stripped off the blue-and-gray striped suit she'd worn to work that morning, took a shower, blew her hair dry, and put on a black crepe pleated skirt that reached to mid-calf and a long sweater of the same color, threaded through with silver. She had just finished applying her makeup when the doorbell rang.

Glory crossed her empty living room and opened the door to admit Jesse, who looked handsome in charcoal slacks and a cream colored fisherman's sweater. He wore a tweed overcoat, too, and his brash brown eyes moved over Glory's figure with undisguised appreciation.

She longed for an excuse to touch him, but there was none. "You look very nice," she said.

There was something wry about his grin. "So do you," he answered.

At first, it was like old times. Jesse helped Glory into her coat and held her elbow protectively as he escorted her to the classic old luxury car parked outside.

"No truck?" Glory teased, as she sank into the cushiony leather seat.

Jesse shut the car door and came around to get behind the wheel before answering. "Nothing but the best for you," he said, and each word was stretched taut, like a violin string.

Heat flowed out of the vehicle's heater, ruffling Glory's thin skirt, and soft music streamed from its impressive stereo system. "Your grandfather's car," she reflected, just to break the silence. "We went to the prom in this car, didn't we?"

She regretted the question instantly.

Jesse's eyes smoldered as he looked at her for a long moment before nodding and pulling away from the curb. They'd made love that night after the dance, and they'd been so excited that they hadn't even taken off all their clothes. Jesse had set Glory astraddle his lap and, gripping her hips, lowered her onto his shaft...

She was desperate, so she tried again. Reaching out to switch off the heat, she asked, "Do you think it's going to keep snowing like this?"

Jesse was no help, at all. "Until February or March, probably. I guess you're not used to it anymore, since you've been living in the western part of the state."

Glory gave a strangled cry of frustration. "Jesse, don't just leave me dangling. I need some assistance here."

He gave her a teasing glance that did as much to ignite her senses as her memories had. His eyes said assistance wasn't what she needed, though his lips moved only to curve into a half grin.

"So, did you win the election by a wide margin, or what?" she threw out, in another wild attempt at normal conversation.

"Were you in love with that guy you left behind in Portland?" he countered out of the blue.

Glory was instantly defensive, and she was grateful for it. "How did you know about Alan?"

"I asked you if you loved him."

"No—yes—I don't know!" How could she say, straight out, that she'd never loved another man besides Jesse himself? "Damn it, this isn't fair. You said we were going to talk about Liza!"

Jesse was shaking his head, and though his tone was polite, his words were downright inflammatory. "At least I know I'm not the only guy you ever ran out on. How many others were there?"

Glory wanted to slug him, but the roads were slick and she couldn't be sure he wouldn't lose control of the car, so she knotted her fists in her lap and savored the fantasy. "Take me home."

"I'll be glad to—at the end of the evening, when we've settled something. Anything."

They were leaving the city limits and climbing along the well-plowed tree-lined highway that led to Fawn Creek. Glory was startled when Jesse pulled the car off the road into a secluded rest area that was familiar for all the wrong reasons.

He shut off the engine and the lights and, after Glory's eyes adjusted, she could see him fairly clearly in the muted glow from the dashboard. "You're driving me crazy," he said, as though that explained everything.

"Start this car this instant," Glory sputtered, on the verge of panic. She was a strong woman, certainly not promiscuous, but Jesse Bainbridge had always been her downfall. "I want to go home."

"I know damn well what you want, and so do you. And maybe we're not going to get anywhere with the rest of our lives until we've taken care of it."

Glory grabbed ineptly at the door handle, but she never made contact. "Jesse, if you force me—"

"I won't have to force you," he pointed out, his fingers resting lightly on the back of her neck. "And we both know it."

He pushed a button somewhere, and the seat back eased slowly downward until she was lying prone. Before she could cope with that development, Jesse was kissing her, and one of his strong hands was resting on her thigh.

He snapped open her seat belt and laid it aside, then went right on kissing her, while his hand moved her skirt slowly upward.

She managed to free her mouth from his, though it didn't like its liberty and wanted to surrender. "Jesse—"

Jesse eased her long, glistening sweater up and over her head, and deftly unfastened the front catch on her bra. He was watching, waiting, when her plump breasts spilled out, their tips already seeking him.

With a husky chuckle, he took one nipple into his mouth, and the sensation made Glory moan aloud and stretch out on the seat in involuntary abandon. His hand found the top of her panty hose and began rolling them slowly and surely downward.

Everything was happening as fast as a sleigh ride down McCalley's Hill, but Glory couldn't put on the brakes. She'd been without Jesse's touch for too long, craved it too desperately.

He found the aching center of her femininity and delved under its mat of silk to the quavering nubbin beneath. Glory groaned again as he rolled her between his fingers.

"Oh, Jesse—" she pleaded.

He bent until his head was lying in her lap, and then his lips and tongue replaced his fingers, and Glory gave a lusty shout and thrust her hips high.

Jesse chuckled against her, but he showed no mercy of any kind. His hands clasped her bottom, and he held her to his tender vengeance, taking everything she had to give. He laid her back on the seat, only to ignite the blazes all over again by sucking at her breasts and stroking them.

When she was twisting beneath his hands and mouth, feverish for the union she knew she should deny herself, he shifted her, so that he was lying on the seat and she was kneeling over him. He opened his slacks and lowered Glory onto him.

Her body surged into reflexive action, but Jesse gripped her hips and measured the pace, whispering ragged, senseless words as he sheathed and unsheathed himself in her.

"Jesse—*Jesse*—" She sought his mouth with hers, and he gave her a brief, fiery kiss. But he was caught up in a tender agony of his own, and he finally thrust his head back and uttered an exclamation.

In the next moment, their bodies made a pact independent of their minds, fusing together in a hot, searing thrust. Glory cried out and arched her back when Jesse intensified every sensation by pulling her forward and catching one of her nipples in his mouth.

When she collapsed against him, she was crying. "Damn you, Jesse," she sobbed brokenly. "Are you satisfied now?"

His chuckle was more tender than amused. "A strangely appropriate question," he gasped. And then he wrapped his arms around Glory and he held her for a long time, until they'd both recovered a little.

Only then did Glory realize that Jesse had shed not only his overcoat but his sweater, too. And her coat was jumbled into a corner with them. It scared her that she didn't remember the process of that.

"Oh, God," she sniffled, as Jesse dislodged himself to pull on his sweater and raise the seat back.

"Glory, it's all right," he rasped, as she dried her eyes with some tissue from the glove compartment and did her best to straighten her clothes.

Glory slammed the glove compartment and snapped her seat belt back into place. "Well, now you've proved it," she said, in a furious, singsong voice riddled with tears. "For a good time, a guy just has to call Glory Parsons!"

He silenced her by taking her chin in his hand. His grasp was hard but not painful. "Don't ever say that again," he bit out. "I made love to you because I wanted to, not because I was trying to make a point!'' He paused to drag in a deep, ragged breath. ''Now, maybe we can concentrate long enough to figure out what the hell we're going to do about our daughter.''

6

Because Jesse insisted, they went on to the restaurant in Fawn Creek, and Glory headed straight for the women's room to make repairs on her hair and makeup. When she came out, Jesse was waiting for her, and his brash brown eyes smiled even though his lips were still.

"Don't worry," he whispered a few moments later, as they followed a waitress to their table. "Nobody would ever guess that half an hour ago you were having your way with me."

Glory's cheeks burned and she glared up at Jesse, her lips drawn tight across her teeth, as he pulled back her chair for her.

"You did all the seducing," she pointed out, once they were alone with their menus and a flickering candle.

Jesse leaned forward in his chair. "Maybe so." He grinned. "But when you got warmed up, you were plenty willing to play the game."

"We came here," Glory reminded him stiffly, snapping her menu open, "to discuss Liza."

"By the way," Jesse began, drawing his eyebrows together briefly in a frown. "Are you doing anything for birth control, or did we just make the same mistake twice?"

Glory gave a hissing sigh and slapped her menu down on the table. "It's so typical of you to ask after the fact. Yes, I've got an IUD. And furthermore, I don't consider Liza a mistake."

"I can see we're going to get a lot settled tonight," Jesse replied through his teeth.

The waitress returned, and they both ordered chicken enchiladas with beans and rice. Glory wondered why they couldn't agree on anything besides food and sex.

Neither of them spoke again until their dinner salads had been delivered.

"I guess things must have been pretty serious between you and that Alan character, if you have an IUD," Jesse commented.

Glory took aim and fired back. "I guess things must be pretty serious between you and Adara, too, since everybody in town knows you bought her an engagement ring for Christmas."

"Adara and I are finished," he said, stabbing at his salad with his fork.

Glory smiled acidly. "What a coincidence. So are Alan and I. So why would we want to talk about them?"

Jesse shrugged and tried to look nonchalant, but Glory wasn't fooled. It troubled his male ego to know she'd had a long-term relationship with another man; Jesse had always been a very proprietary animal.

"I think you should tell Liza you're her father," Glory ventured to say, long minutes later, when their dinners had arrived. "I mean, it must have been hard on her, losing Gresham and Sandy."

Jesse sighed, and the look in his eyes was, for a moment, grievously sad. "It was," he said gravely. "I don't mind admitting I had some trouble with it myself. Gresh was busy with politics, even when I was a kid, but he always had time for me."

A knot formed in Glory's throat. She knew how close a person could be to his brother, and how much it hurt to lose him. A part of her was still standing beside Dylan's grave, watching in numb disbelief as they lowered his coffin into the ground, aching because a stupid mistake on another airman's part had robbed him of his life. She nodded, because that was all she could manage.

Accurately reading the expression on her face, Jesse reached out and closed his hand over hers. "If Gresh and Dylan were here," he said quietly, "they'd tell us to stop worrying over the dead and think about the living."

Glory nodded again. "I know."

Over coffee, Jesse was the one to bring up the subject of their daughter. "Why is it so important to you that I tell Liza I'm her father?"

It was a question Glory had thoroughly examined in her own mind. "Kids tend to find out things like that. And when they do, they're devastated because nobody told them the truth."

He arched one eyebrow. "No ulterior motives? Like wanting her to put two and two together and decide that if I'm her father, you must be her mother?"

Glory met his gaze steadily. "I'd love for Liza to know who I am, under the right circumstances. But I care more about her happiness and welfare."

At that, Jesse looked skeptical, and their brief, tenuous truce was over. "Either that, or you have a rich relative somewhere, and the only way you can inherit is by proving you've produced offspring."

Even though his expression had forewarned her, Jesse's words still came as a slap in the face. "Did I hurt you that much?" she asked, when she'd gotten her breath back.

"Yes," he answered coldly. "I was eighteen, Glory, and gullible as hell. You'd told me with words and with your body that you loved me.

When you ran off without telling me why it was over, the pain was so bad that I couldn't stand still. When I tried, it consumed me like fire.

"I did everything I knew to find you, but nobody wanted to help me, including Dylan and your mother." He paused, and his eyes, averted from Glory's face, were haunted. "I'll never forget the day I finally had to give up. Gresh had taken me fishing, trying to snap me out of it. He said if I didn't tell somebody about my feelings, they'd never go away, they'd just get worse. I threw my fishing pole down and yelled, it hurt so much. When Gresh put his arms around me, I cried like a two-year-old."

Glory had seen the images vividly in her mind as Jesse was talking, and she ached. Driven to distraction by her own pain, she'd inflicted agony on a person she loved with her whole heart. "I don't suppose it would help to say that I'm sorry, that I was hurting, too?"

Jesse threw two bills down onto the table to cover the cost of their meal and shoved back his chair. His eyes were hot with remembered frustration, as Glory stood with him. "Maybe someday it will," he responded in a low voice. "Right now, I feel like it all happened last Tuesday."

At the coatrack beside the restaurant's front door, he settled Glory's coat on her shoulders, then shrugged into his own. Although he was unfailingly polite, linking her arm with his so she wouldn't fall in the icy parking lot, opening the car door for her, something in his manner chilled Glory through and through.

Shame all but crushed her as she realized that, whatever he'd said to the contrary, Jesse had made love to her that night to avenge himself. He didn't care for her, and probably hadn't even especially wanted her. God knew, Jesse could have had just about any single woman in Pearl River County for the asking.

"We should have left well enough alone, Jesse, and stayed away from each other," she said miserably, when he brought the elegant old car to a stop in front of her building.

He was staring straight over the wheel instead of looking at her, and his profile was rigid. "I tried to tell you that," he answered gruffly after a long, difficult interval. His brown eyes were full of accusations when he turned to her. "For your own sake, Glory, and for Liza's and mine, please let this thing alone. Go back to Portland and your boyfriend and forget we made a baby ten years ago."

Glory's eyes filled with tears. In a way, she thought Jesse was right, she should go, but she knew even then that she wouldn't be able to make herself do it. The knowledge of Liza's existence would haunt her for the rest of her life.

"If you and I never exchange another civil word," she said, unfastening her seat belt and pushing open the car door, "it'll be all right. But I can't leave my daughter. I won't."

She was halfway up the walk when Jesse caught up with her and forcefully took her arm. The irony of it would have made her laugh out loud, if she hadn't been in so much emotional pain. The sheriff of Pearl River County didn't mind ripping out her heart and stomping on it, but he'd be damned if he'd let a lady walk to her door unescorted!

She shoved the key into the lock and would have gone inside without another word, if Jesse hadn't grasped her shoulders and forced her to face him.

"Damn it, Glory," he breathed, his jaw set so tightly it was a wonder he could speak at all, "leave Liza alone! I don't want her in pieces, when you decide you're bored with Pearl River and need to move on!"

Glory longed to slap him, but her fury was too great. It practically paralyzed her. "Sorry, Sheriff," she told him, "but I'm going to be a part of the landscape around here, and you'd damn well better get used to it!" With that, she shoved open the door.

Jesse yelled a swear word, heedless of the neighbors, shoved his hands into the pockets of his expensive overcoat and stalked back to his car.

All night long, Jesse tossed and turned, alternately burning to feel Glory beneath him, receiving him, and wanting to strangle her. She was like a fever beginning in his brain and spreading into his body, destroying his reason, changing him from a man of the nineties to a cave dweller.

After a shower and a haphazard shave, Jesse put on his uniform and called the office to let them know where to find him. And then he got into his truck, backed it out of the driveway, and practically floorboarded the gas pedal.

The vehicle fishtailed on the blindingly white packed snow as he drove toward the main road.

A left turn would have taken him into Pearl River, but Jesse turned right. He stopped once to use the winch on his truck to pull a young couple's car out of the ditch.

No one was hurt, but they had a baby with them, and the weather was colder than a witch's nipple. Jesse made sure the old heap they were driving would run before going on.

In a way, he envied those two kids their youth and innocence, as well as the unique young life they'd created together. He hoped they knew they were rich, even if they couldn't afford a decent rig, and that they would fight to hold on to what they had when they hit the inevitable white water.

He set his teeth. At that age, he would have fought any force in the universe to keep Glory and their child at his side—if he'd been given the option.

He was grateful when Twin Poplars Convalescent Home loomed up in the distance; he'd spent the night thinking about Glory, and he needed a distraction.

Vicky Walters, a nurse Jesse had dated briefly before he and Adara had started seeing each other, greeted him with a smile. Only then did it strike him that she bore a faint resemblance, with her blond hair and blue eyes, to Glory.

"Hi, Jesse. Nasty morning out, isn't it?"

He grinned and shivered in reply. "Speaking of nasty, is my grandfather up?"

Vicky laughed. "He's already had his breakfast, and he happens to be in a pretty good mood. He was in his room last time I saw him."

Jesse's grin faded as soon as he got past Vicky. Even on his best days, Seth Bainbridge wasn't an easy man to deal with. And this sure as hell wasn't going to be one of his best days.

Seth sat at the window, slumped in his wheelchair, dressed in his robe and slippers and gazing out from beneath bushy eyebrows at the dazzlingly white world. He still had his hair, though it was mostly gray now, and his eyes were as sharp as ever, like his mind. But the rest of his body had betrayed him by turning feeble.

"Gramps?" Jesse paused in the doorway, his hands braced on either side of the jamb.

The old man wheeled around and scowled at him. "Hello, Jesse."

"Can I come in, or do I have to get a warrant?" Jesse asked, trying to smile. It was tough to keep up a front sometimes, because the old cuss could be so hard and cold. And this was one of his *good* days.

"Come in," the judge grumbled, waving one hand in a desultory gesture. "Come in."

Even after he'd crossed the threshold, Jesse couldn't make himself sit. "How have you been feeling?"

"Like hell," the old man answered gruffly.

Jesse drew in a deep breath, let it out slowly. He had to go carefully here; he didn't want to cause the judge to have another stroke. And yet there were things he needed to know. "Glory Parsons is back in town." He said the words with the same caution he would have used to make sure the ice over Culley's Creek was thick enough to hold his weight.

He'd expected a reaction, and he got one. Seth's gaze snapped to his face and narrowed there, and his gnarled hands clenched on the arms of his chair. "That cheap, lying, little—"

Jesse had a lot of unresolved issues where Glory was concerned himself, but he wasn't about to let the judge insult her. "Hold it," he said firmly, raising both hands, palms out. "I don't want a dose of your venom, Gramps, and I swear to God I'll walk out of here and never come back if you don't watch your mouth."

Seth had few enough visitors, Jesse suspected, because when it came right down to it, he didn't have any friends, at all, except for old Doc Cupples. As for family, Gresham and Sandy were dead, of course, and he'd long since alienated Ilene with his black moods. She refused to subject Liza to the old man's unpredictable temperament, and Jesse backed her up on the decision.

Which left himself and the aging doctor as the only people who ever paid a call of any kind.

"All right," Seth muttered. He was silent for a long time, then he went on. "She shouldn't have come back. She promised she wouldn't."

Jesse's fist knotted; he wanted to slam it down on the dresser top, hard enough to make lamps and ashtrays jump, but he restrained himself. "So you did send her away," he ground out.

"Sit down," fussed the old man. "It hurts my neck to look up at you like that."

Jesse dragged a chair over and sank into it. "All right, you old reprobate, start talking."

"She would have ruined your life," his grand-father insisted. And had Seth been able to close his hands into fists, Jesse figured he would have. As it was, agitation was clearly written in every line of his body. "You wouldn't have gone to college. By God, you wouldn't be sheriff today, with every prospect of entering the state legislature in a few years!"

Jesse rubbed his eyes with a thumb and forefinger and sighed. "Glory was pregnant with my baby, wasn't she? And you ran her off because of your damn family pride."

"The baby was yours," Seth agreed bitterly. "I knew that the moment I saw Liza. But she *could* have belonged to anybody in the county!"

"Watch it," Jesse warned, his voice as rough as two rusty nails being rubbed together. In that moment, Jesse realized that he'd suspected Glory's pregnancy all along; he'd just never been able to get anybody to confirm it.

Seth trembled with frustration and rage and the relative inability to express those emotions. "Glory Parsons wasn't like Gresham's Sandy—she didn't come from a good family. That brother of hers was practically a criminal, and as for her mother—"

"Glory was as good as anybody, Gramps," Jesse interrupted in an angry undertone, "and *better* than you and I put together. Dylan was no worse than any of the rest of us, and let's not mince words here—you didn't like Delphine because you wanted to sleep with her and she told you to go to hell."

For a long time, Seth just sat there, gripping the arms of his chair and swallowing repeatedly. Finally he ground out, "I did the right thing, Jesse. Gresham and Sandy wanted a baby, and I made sure they got one. And I saved you from the mistake of a lifetime, you ungrateful young whelp!"

Jesse rose from the chair, went into the bathroom, and drew a glass of cold water for his grandfather. Seth was still red in the face when he got back. "Take it easy," Jesse said, holding out the glass.

Seth obviously would have liked to knock the cup out of Jesse's hand, but he didn't because he needed the water to steady himself. He drank it down thirstily. "I paid her to leave," he muttered, and the words were ugly to Jesse, even though he'd long since guessed that Glory had sold him out for money.

Hearing the words from his grandfather lifted them out of the realm of theory and planted them squarely in reality. And they were wounding. He averted his eyes to a naked tree beyond the window, but the old man was ruthless. He knew he'd cornered his prey, and he couldn't resist closing in for the kill.

"She could have come to you, Jesse, and told you about the baby. You would have married her. But we both know why she didn't, don't we? Because I told her I'd cut you off without a nickel the day you put a ring on her finger, and she didn't want you *or* the baby if she couldn't have the Bainbridge money, too."

Jesse thrust himself out of the chair and turned his back. He felt broken inside, just the way he had that long-ago summer day when Dylan had told him Glory had gone away and wasn't ever coming back. Only now he didn't have Gresh to help him get his balance back. He didn't have anybody.

"You ought to be thanking me on your knees!" the old man went on, tearing at Jesse's spirit like a frenzied shark. "*I saved you* from that calculating little tease!"

Not trusting himself to speak, Jesse strode out of the room, his grandfather's bitter words ringing in his ears.

On her lunch hour, Glory left the bank and drove cautiously along the icy roads until she reached the Pearl River cemetery. Then, parking her car outside the gates, she made her way on foot to Dylan's grave.

The headstone was mounded with snow, but the letters of his name were clearly visible. Glory sniffled and shoved her hands into the pockets of her coat. Then, after looking around to make sure she was alone, she started talking.

"Last night Jesse and I went out to dinner," she said, pulling one mittened hand out to wipe her eyes. "We took that fancy old car that belongs to his grandfather and—well—we ended up making love on the seat like a couple of teenagers." Glory paused to sniffle again. "Actually, it wouldn't classify as lovemaking, given the fact that Jesse was just trying to get back at me for hurting him. The Anglo-Saxon term would fit better, but you know me—I can't say that because I think it's so ugly."

An icy breeze swept in among the naked trees, ruffling Glory's hair and stinging her ears. She tried to imagine what Dylan would say if he were there, and it wasn't difficult. He'd have vowed to find Jesse Bainbridge and loosen a few of his teeth.

"Violence won't solve anything, Dylan," she said firmly.

She guessed that then he would have put an arm around her shoulders and told her not to be so hard on herself, that everybody makes mistakes.

"Thanks," she snuffled. Then she took one of the small candy canes the bank was giving away from her purse, stuck it like a little flag in the snow on top of Dylan's headstone, and carefully returned to her car.

She got back to the bank just in time for a staff meeting, and the rest of the afternoon was so busy that quitting time came long before she expected it.

Not wanting to go home to her apartment and sit in a folding chair, staring at a blank wall, Glory went to the diner instead. Delphine was off-duty, and her daughter found her upstairs, curled up on the couch with a romance novel.

"Hi," Glory said brightly. And then she promptly burst into tears.

"I'd ask what's bothering you," Delphine said with gentle wryness, patting her daughter on the back, "but I already know it's Jesse. Sit down, and I'll get you a nice hot cup of tea to settle your nerves."

Glory collapsed into a chair without even bothering to take off her coat, and let her purse tumble to the floor. "He hates me," she said, resting one elbow on the arm of the chair and propping her forehead in her palm.

"Nonsense," replied Delphine from the kitchenette. "He just wants your body, and it's making him crazy."

Glory let out a despairing wail. "He's already had my body!" she sobbed.

Diplomatically, Delphine waited a few beats before responding to that. "I take it we're not talking about ten years ago, when you were young, foolish and hormonal."

"We're talking about *last night*!" Glory ranted.

"Good grief," Delphine muttered, materializing at her side with a glass of water and two aspirin tablets. "Get a grip before you give yourself a headache."

Glory swallowed the aspirin and felt a little better just for having been fussed over. "This would all be so much easier if it weren't for Jesse."

"None of this would have *happened* if it weren't for Jesse." She patted Glory's shoulder distractedly. "Honey, please don't tell me you've come up with some crazy plan to replace Liza by getting pregnant with Jesse's baby all over again."

"Of course I haven't!" Glory cried, getting awkwardly out of her coat and leaving it all bunched up in the chair behind her.

Delphine returned to the stove as the tea kettle began to whistle. "Well, then, how did it happen?"

"I've never been like this with any other man," she marveled furiously. "But for some reason all Jesse has to do is kiss me and I go absolutely wild."

The older woman arched one auburn eyebrow as she handed Glory her cup of tea and then sat down to face her. "You know," she said, her eyes twinkling with mischief as she tapped the cover of her romance novel, "Storm Ravenbrook is having the same problem with her man, if it's any comfort to you."

"It isn't," Glory assured her huffily.

Delphine sighed. "Sweetheart, I warned you about staying here in Pearl River. To quote those old western movies on TV, this town just ain't big enough for the two of you. And since Jesse owns a mansion, the sawmill, and half the real estate in the county, he isn't very likely to move on. That means—"

"I know, I know," Glory interrupted wearily, taking a somewhat unladylike sip of her tea. "I've either got to leave or learn to deal with our illustrious sheriff."

"That's about the size of it," Delphine agreed. Having listened to people's problems at the diner for so long, she'd probably heard more sad stories than the average psycho-therapist. Her basic philosophy was that ninety-seven percent of life was just a matter of showing up, and the other three consisted of rolling with the punches.

"Thanks, Mama," Glory said.

"What for?"

"For not judging me. Until they start a group called Jesse Anonymous, I'm afraid I'm going to have to play this thing by ear."

Delphine laughed. "In your case, I think the affliction may be incurable. Has it ever occurred to you, my darling daughter, that you might still be in love with the man?"

Glory's eyes went wide with alarm at the suggestion. As much as she thought about Jesse, as wantonly as she'd behaved in his arms the night before, the possibility had never crossed her mind.

"No," she said. *"No!"*

Delphine just shrugged and asked Glory if she wanted to stay for dinner. Harold, who was working on a plumbing job in Fawn Creek, was going to stop off on the way home and pick up a big pepperoni pizza.

Glory shook her head and gathered her crumpled coat around her. "I'd just be a drag," she said. Then she stood, bending to kiss Delphine's forehead. "Thanks for everything, Mama. I love you."

Delphine squeezed her hand. "If you decide you want to talk some more or just hang around, I'll be right here until about eight o'clock. Then Harold and I are going over to the new house to put shelf paper in the cupboards."

Glory promised to seek her mother out if she hit another crisis, and left. She was walking back to the bank parking lot, where her car was waiting, when Ilene came out of the bookstore and waved.

"You look half frozen," the woman called. "Come on over, and Liza and I will thaw you out."

After the last twenty-four hours, the offer of time with Liza was irresistible. Glory looked both ways and then hurried across the icy street and into the bookstore.

A lush-looking artificial tree had been set up in one corner of the shop, which was now closed for the day. Lights were strung among the branches, and Liza was decorating the boughs with old-fashioned glass ornaments.

"Hi, Glory," she chimed with a smile that pulled at Glory's insides and almost brought tears to her eyes.

Glory hid her reaction by taking off her coat and hanging it up. "Hi, there," she finally answered, when she was a little more composed. "That's a pretty tree."

"Thank you," Liza replied. "Aunt Ilene says cutting down a live one is senseless slaughter. Uncle Jesse always gets a big spruce for the big house, though."

Amusement at Liza's vernacular saved Glory from flinching, at least inwardly, at the mention of Jesse. The twinkling colored lights on the tree cheered her a little, and she carefully picked up an ornament and handed it to the child.

Liza hung the piece from a branch and looked up at Glory with Christmas reflected on her earnest little face. "Will you stay for supper, Glory? Aunt Ilene said it was all right to invite you, and we're having Chinese."

Glory glanced at Ilene, who smiled and nodded. "I'd like that very much," she said softly, reaching out one hand to touch her child and then drawing it back at the last moment. Embarrassed, she turned to Ilene again. "Is there anything I can do to help?"

Ilene's expression was one of tender understanding. "Just keep this young lady company," she said, gesturing toward Liza, "while I deep-fry the wontons." With that, she turned and left the shop for the apartment upstairs.

"Aunt Ilene's a good cook," Liza confided. "She thinks trying foods from other countries will promote peace, so we eat lots of strange stuff."

Glory smiled and began decorating the top portion of the tree, where Liza couldn't reach. The activity was so ordinary—parents and children did this everywhere, every year—but to Glory it was precious. "What are you asking Santa for?" she inquired casually, not sure whether her daughter believed or not.

"Santa's really Uncle Jesse," Liza confided, leaning close to whisper the words gently, lest they come as a terrible shock. "And I already got what I want."

"What was that?" Glory asked, her voice hoarse because of the lump in her throat.

"For Uncle Jesse not to get married to Adara."

"Don't you like her?"

"I like her all right. I just don't think she's Uncle Jesse's type."

Glory smiled. "I see."

"I want somebody who'll bring cookies to school and come in my room and hug me if I have a bad dream—like Mommy used to do."

Glory's heart twisted, and before she thought, she leaned down and kissed Liza on the crown of her head, just where her bright-penny hair was parted. When she straightened, she saw Jesse standing on the other side of the store's front window, glaring at her.

7

The bell over the bookshop door didn't jingle merrily as Jesse came in; it jangled in warning.

"Uncle Jesse!" Liza whooped, flinging herself at the man, apparently never noticing his taciturn expression.

Looking on in silence, Glory envied Jesse the child's wild affection.

"Hi, Button," Jesse answered distractedly, hugging the nine-year-old and then giving one of her braids a little tug. His eyes never left Glory's face the whole time, and their expression wasn't friendly.

She was saved from having to speak to him, at least temporarily, when Ilene appeared, pushing up the sleeves of her bright purple sweater and smiling.

"Hello, Jesse. Want to join us for supper? We're having Chinese."

He rubbed his chin, which was showing a stubble of beard, and at last he turned from Glory. He smiled at his cousin. "No thanks," he answered. "I'm still on duty." He looked down at Liza's face then, and now it was as though Glory were invisible to him. "I'm going out looking for a Christmas tree this Saturday, and I'd like you to come along if you want to."

"Yes!" Liza cried, and her eagerness made Glory's heart constrict. "I want to! Could Glory come with us, please? And Aunt Ilene?"

"Saturday's my busiest day, what with Christmas coming on," Ilene interceded with a gentle shake of her head.

Glory stood awkwardly by, embarrassed, not knowing what to say. It was obvious Jesse hadn't intended to include her in the invitation, and she could have gotten off the hook by saying she had to do her holiday shopping that day. But the painful truth was that she wanted, just once, to go on a Christmas-tree-hunting expedition with her daughter and the man who had fathered her.

Jesse narrowed his eyes at Glory, as though he suspected her of making Liza ask to bring her along by ventriloquism, but then he said grudgingly, "I guess it would be all right."

Liza cheered and hugged Jesse again, then scrambled upstairs to get something she wanted to show him. Diplomatically, Ilene went along.

"What are you doing here?" Jesse immediately demanded, placing his hands on his hips.

Glory stepped away from the artificial Christmas tree, realizing only then that she'd unconsciously been trying to hide among its branches. She sighed. "What does it look like I'm doing here, Jesse? I'm spending time with Liza."

He lifted one finger and shook it at her, starting to speak, but Liza reappeared before he got a word out.

"Here it is, Uncle Jesse," she burst out, waving a sheet of paper. "It's my math assignment. I got an *A*."

Jesse grinned. "That's great," he said, taking the child's eager offering. "Can I keep it? I'd like to pin it up on the bulletin board at my office, so all the deputies will know what a smart kid I've—you are."

Liza was beaming. "Okay," she said. And then she turned her bright green eyes to Glory. "Supper's ready. Aunt Ilene said to lock the door after Uncle Jesse and come up."

With a chuckle, Jesse bent to kiss Liza's forehead. "See you tomorrow, kid," he said. After that, he exchanged a brief look with Glory, silently warning her not to overstep her bounds.

She responded with a grudging nod, and he went out.

That night when dinner was over Glory helped Liza with the dishes and her homework, then read her a chapter of *Little House in the Big Woods* before tucking her into bed. When she'd kissed the child good-night and closed the door of her small room, she sought out Ilene, who was at the kitchen table, tallying the day's receipts for the bookshop.

"Thank you," Glory said.

Ilene gestured toward the colorful teapot in the center of the table with a smile. "Help yourself," she said. "It's herbal, so it won't keep you awake."

Since Ilene had also set out a cup, Glory poured some tea and took a sip. "Why are you so kind to me?" she asked, in a voice carefully modulated not to carry as far as Liza's room. "I mean, I'm a stranger as far as you're concerned."

"I have good instincts about people," Ilene said. "Besides, I believe in families."

Glory swallowed. She simply wasn't up to the topic of families, not after an evening of emotional ups and downs that had left her slightly disoriented and tired to the center of her heart.

Ilene patted her hand. "You've got good instincts, too, Glory," she said softly. "And you loved Jesse once. If you'll just give him time, he'll come to terms with all of this and start behaving like a human being again."

That brought a wan smile from Glory. "I hope you're right," she sighed, "because it will be very hard to have a relationship with Liza, if Jesse and I can't get along."

After that, the two women drank tea and talked about other Christmases, in other places. Glory was tired and pleasantly relaxed when she left to fetch her car from the bank's parking lot and drive the rest of the way home.

"I guess you've done all the thinking you need to do," Adara said, accurately guessing the reason for Jesse's unscheduled visit. He wanted to leave it at that, to get back into his patrol car and drive away, but his sense of honor wouldn't permit such an easy out.

He entered Adara's apartment when she stepped back to admit him. "I'm sorry," he said, standing there in the middle of her living room, shoving his hands into the pockets of his jacket.

The tears shimmering in her eyes filled him with guilt, because he knew she would have done anything to hold them back.

"It's Glory?" she asked with a despairing lilt in her voice.

Jesse raised his shoulders in a shrug. "I'm not sure. The situation is pretty complicated."

Adara nodded. "I imagine so. Five people must have come into the shop today just to tell me that you took her to dinner last night."

"I'm sorry," Jesse said again. The reminder of the night before, when he and Glory had made love, would be sweet torment for some time to come. He supposed he deserved it.

He went to the door, and Adara followed, speaking quickly. "If you're not happy with her—"

Jesse touched her lips with the tips of his fingers. "Don't say it," he replied quietly. And then he left Adara's apartment for the last time.

On Wednesday, the movers stopped at the bank to inform Glory that her furniture and other belongings had arrived, and Mr. Baker gave her the rest of the day off to get things squared away. The moment the movers were gone, she unearthed her espresso maker and brewed herself a *latte*.

She was sipping the mixture of espresso and steamed milk and trying to decide which carton to unpack first, when her doorbell chimed. Expecting Delphine, or perhaps Jill, Glory was surprised to find Liza standing in the hallway, looking slightly ill-at-ease.

Glory never laid eyes on the child without a painful tug at her heart, but she was ready with a smile. "Hi," she said warmly, stepping back so that Liza could come in.

"Hi," Liza answered, stepping over the threshold and then just standing there in her little coat and boots, shifting back and forth from one foot to the other.

"Does your Aunt Ilene know where you are?" Glory asked, reaching out gently to unbutton Liza's coat.

Liza nodded. "I told her. She has a migraine headache and had to go upstairs and lie down."

Glory was concerned. "Is there anything I can do for her?"

Liza shook her head and tugged off her mittens and stocking cap, all of which Glory laid aside with the coat. "Nothing works but peace and quiet. I'm supposed to wait at the sheriff's office and have supper with Uncle Jesse tonight."

"Did you call him from school?" Glory inquired, wending her way through the stacks of boxes to the kitchen, where she planned to make hot cocoa for Liza.

"No," Liza replied nervously. "He's probably out chasing criminals, anyway. I'll go straight to the office after I leave here."

"I think we'd better call him," Glory said.

Liza stopped her by grasping her hand. "First I have to ask you something."

A chill went through Glory, followed by a wild hope that this bright, perceptive child had already figured out the secret she and Jesse were keeping from her. "Yes?"

"Do you sew in this lifetime?"

Glory chuckled, at once relieved and disappointed. "Yes, a little. Why?"

"Because I'm going to be the only angel in the pageant without a costume if I don't get somebody to help me," Liza blurted out. "Uncle Jesse's got something on his mind—he doesn't even hear half the questions I ask him—and Aunt Ilene used to be a seamstress in France, during a war. It was an unhappy life, and she swears she'll never pick up another needle and thread—"

Glory resisted an impulse to hug the child and laughed softly. "Sure I'll help you. Do you have the directions?"

Liza nodded and threw her arms around Glory. "Oh, thank you!" she cried. While Glory was recovering from that, the little girl hurried to her coat and extracted a folded, much-worried-over piece of paper containing basic instructions and a list of materials for an angel costume.

"The first thing we have to do," Glory reflected, reading over the paper, "is call your Uncle Jesse and let him know exactly where you are. Then we'll drive to Fawn Creek and get the materials we need."

Liza's green eyes were alight at the prospect. "The mall will be all decorated for Christmas!"

Glory nodded, smiling, and went to the telephone affixed to her kitchen wall. After asking Liza for the number, she called the sheriff's department, identified herself and politely asked for Jesse.

Another voice came on the line. "Glory? This is Deputy Johnson. Jesse's out on a call right now. Can I help you?"

Twisting the cord around her finger, Glory frowned. She would have preferred to relay the message directly to Jesse, so there could be no mistake, but she couldn't wait. She'd gotten Liza all excited about the project. "Just tell him, please, that Liza is with me. We'll be out of town for a while, picking up some things in Fawn Creek."

"I'll make sure he knows," Deputy Johnson promised earnestly.

Glory thanked him and hung up. In the process of preparing Liza and then herself for the cold, she forgot Jesse even existed. She couldn't remember the last time she'd looked forward to anything as much as she did those few stolen hours with her child.

The two of them had just passed the city limits in Glory's sports car, happily singing Christmas carols, when a siren sounded behind them and blue-and-red lights flashed ominously in the rearview mirror.

Knowing she hadn't been speeding, Glory frowned as she pulled over to the side of the road.

It shouldn't have surprised her, she guessed, that the officer who strode up beside her car was Jesse.

She rolled down her window and opened her mouth, but he didn't give her a chance to speak.

"Get out of the car," he ordered in an undertone that, for all its even meter, was girded in steel.

Glory glanced at Liza and smiled to reassure the child, who looked surprised and worried. "It's okay, honey," she said. "Your Uncle Jesse obviously didn't get the message that we left, so he and I have to talk."

Liza looked relieved. "Hi, Uncle Jesse," she sang out, wiggling her fingers.

He managed a semblance of a smile, and even though his eyes were hidden behind mirrored sunglasses, Glory knew they were snapping with controlled fury. "Hi," he replied.

Glory opened the door and stepped out onto the snowy roadside, and Jesse immediately gripped her by the elbow and hustled her around to the back of the car.

"Where the hell were you taking her?" he demanded in a hiss, as Glory wrenched free of his grasp.

Outraged, Glory folded her arms and rolled her eyes. "To China, Jesse," she answered. "We were making a break for it!" She flung her hands out at her sides and then slapped them against her thighs. "Too bad you had to catch us."

"Do you know how scared I was, when I couldn't find her?" Jesse rasped.

Glory found it only too easy to put herself into Jesse's shoes, and she relented a little. "I'm sorry," she said grudgingly. "Liza came by my apartment and asked me if I'd help with her angel costume. I called your office—I swear it—and left a message with Deputy Johnson that Liza and I were going to the mall in Fawn Creek to buy materials."

He turned away for a moment, his hands resting on his hips, seemingly taking a great interest in the snow-draped pine trees along the road. Glory knew he was composing himself.

Finally he looked at her again. "I thought you were leaving town on the spur of the moment, like before," he confessed. "And taking Liza with you."

It was a marvel that she'd been so angry with Jesse only a moment ago, when now all she wanted to do was comfort him. She wedged her hands into the pockets of her black corduroy pants so she wouldn't lay them on his broad shoulders. "Jesse, I'm not a scared eighteen-year-old girl, anymore. I'm not going to vanish, and I'd never, *never* put you or anyone else through the kind of anguish stealing a child would cause."

He faced her with a heavy sigh and shoved one hand through his hair. "Have her back in time for supper," he said. "And be careful. The roads are slick."

Glory smiled. Ilene had expressed the hope that Jesse would turn back into a human being, and it did seem that he was making noticeable progress toward that end. "You'd better go and tell Liza it's all right," she said, gesturing toward the passenger side of the car, "or she'll worry the whole time we're gone. Pleasing you is important to her, Jesse."

He gave her a look that might have contained a modicum of amused chagrin, shoved his hands into his jacket pockets, and proceeded to Liza's window.

"Have a good time, kid," Glory heard him say, as she rounded the car to get behind the wheel again. The lights on top of Jesse's patrol car were still splashing patches of blue and red over the snow.

"Were we going too fast?" Liza asked, with innocent concern, as she and Glory pulled back onto the highway. In the rearview mirror, Glory could see Jesse standing there at the side of the road, watching them go from behind those damnable sunglasses of his.

Glory shook her head. "He didn't get the message we left for him, so he was worried. Sometimes when parents—*people*—are scared, they act the same way they would if they were angry."

Liza nodded thoughtfully. "Then Gramps must be scared all the time," she reflected. "He's always mad."

"Gramps?" Glory asked, before it came to her that Liza was talking about old Seth Bainbridge, Jesse's grandfather. The hatred she'd always felt for the man seemed to ebb away, leaving sadness and pity in its wake.

"His son was Daddy and Uncle Jesse's father," Liza explained in that amusingly adult manner she sometimes assumed.

The reference to Jesse's brother as "Daddy," indirect as it was, reminded Glory that her gain was Gresham and Sandy's loss, and she wished there was a way to promise them that she'd keep their memories alive in Liza's mind if she could. After all, for six of the little girl's nine years, they'd loved and taken care of her.

"I miss my mommy and daddy a lot at this time of the year," Liza said with a little sigh.

Glory's eyes burned, and she reached out to touch Liza's knee briefly. "I knew your daddy, though not very well." She thought of how Gresham had comforted Jesse after Seth had driven her out of town all those years before. "He was a nice man. Strong, with a ready smile."

Liza giggled. "He used to chase me around the house trying to tickle me," she said.

From then until they reached the mall at Fawn Creek, Glory kept the conversation turning around Gresham and Sandy, and talking about them seemed to be a great relief to Liza. The words and memories, mostly happy, bubbled out of her.

At the mall, Glory bought cups of cocoa for them both, and they sat at a table on the concourse, planning their strategy.

The stores were decorated, and Christmas music was being piped in over a sound system. Although she'd been something of a Scrooge for the past few years, embittered by her breakup with Jesse, the loss of her child and Dylan's subsequent death, Glory found herself getting into the spirit as she and Liza went from shop to shop.

Mindful of Jesse's edict that she have Liza back in Pearl River in time for supper, Glory didn't linger as long as she would have liked. Snowflakes were falling like big feathers shaken from a goose-down pillow, when the two shoppers left the mall with the makings of an angel costume.

It wasn't hard to find Jesse when they got back to town; his patrol car was parked in front of Delphine's diner, and he was standing at the jukebox when Glory and Liza came in.

"I'm going to be the best angel there ever was!" Liza crowed, hurrying to his side and waving the bagful of supplies.

Glory lingered just inside the doorway, very much aware of being outside the circle again. "If Liza could stop by tomorrow sometime, after I get home from work, I'll be able to get started on the costume."

Jesse was holding Liza close against his side, as though he feared to let go, and he didn't look at Glory. "You'll have to talk with Ilene about that," he answered.

After coming close enough to reclaim the shopping bag, Glory turned on one heel, her vision blurred, and hurried out of the diner into the cold and snowy night.

"How come you don't like Glory?" Liza asked, an hour later, when she and Jesse were seated at the table in the mansion's immense dining room, eating her favorite meal of chicken from a bucket.

It occurred to Jesse to hedge, of course, but then he had a strange feeling, as though Gresh were standing in the room with them, urging him to say the right things. He rubbed the back of his neck with one hand. "It isn't that I don't like her, Button."

"You used to be her boyfriend," Liza announced, reaching for a drumstick. "I've seen pictures in your yearbook, and you and Glory were *kissing*."

Jesse chuckled, though he felt sad to the very core of his being. "Yeah. We used to *kiss*," he retorted good-naturedly. "So what?"

"Did you love her?"

He tried hard, but he found that he couldn't lie. "Yes, Captain Quiz, I loved her. Is there anything else you'd like to know?"

Liza caught him off guard by nodding and saying seriously, "Yes. I'd like to know who had me before I got adopted by Mommy and Daddy."

Jesse looked away. So, she was back on that again. He'd hoped the phase was over. "Does it matter? Your mom and dad loved you a whole lot, and they did all the important stuff."

Liza's tone was solemn. "It matters. Someday, I'm going to find my real mom."

"Sandy Bainbridge was your real mom," Jesse said, and though he didn't mean for it to be, his tone was on the sharp side.

His daughter's large green eyes were filled with lingering grief. Maybe it was worse for her at Christmas, knowing Gresh and Sandy were gone forever, like it was for him.

"I just want to ask my mom why she gave me up," she said with gentle defiance, and her lower lip quivered.

Jesse sighed and shoved his paper plate away, then braced his folded arms against the edge of the table. "She was a kid, Liza. She gave you up because she didn't know how to take care of you."

"Gramps told me once that she was eighteen," Liza argued. "Women get married and have babies at that age all the time."

Tonight, of all nights, she had to go into her forty-year-old-midget-posing-as-a-kid routine. "Trust me." Jesse sighed, before slurping up a drink of soda through his straw. "Your mom wasn't mature enough to take care of a baby."

"Did she have a husband?"

"No. I mean, probably not."

Liza narrowed her eyes. "You know what I think, Uncle Jesse? I think you know who my mom is."

How the hell was he supposed to look the kid in the face and deny that? He stood and started gathering up the debris of their dinner, carefully avoiding Liza's gaze. "How would I know that?" he snapped, turning and striding off into the kitchen.

He could feel Liza's suspicious stare following him.

Jesse didn't come back until he'd stood gripping the edge of a counter for nearly five minutes, trying to compose himself. The fact that none of this would be happening if Glory had just stayed in Portland where she belonged did nothing to improve his mood.

When he returned to the dining room, Liza had her school books and a bunch of papers spread out on the table. Jesse was infinitely grateful that the topic of parenthood had been set aside, at least for the moment.

The telephone rang just as they were working the last fraction problem, and Jesse went to the sideboard for the extension. "Bainbridge," he answered, expecting the caller to be someone at the office.

"Jesse, it's Ilene," his cousin said. "The headache isn't improving. Could you please keep Liza tonight?"

Despite his discomfort over the secret he was keeping from Liza, he liked the idea of their being like a real family, at least for one night. "Sure. But maybe I should call Doc Cupples and send him over to have a look at you."

"That old quack?" Ilene retorted. "I wouldn't let him clip my toenails. Besides, I know I'll be better by morning."

"Call if you need anything," Jesse instructed. Then he said goodbye to his cousin and hung up. "Ilene wants you to sleep here tonight," he told Liza. "She's still not feeling well."

Liza relaxed visibly, and Jesse realized she'd been expecting bad news. It broke his heart that the kid was only nine years old and already trained in the adult art of bracing herself against tragedy. "Maybe she needs to go to the hospital."

Jesse kissed the top of his daughter's head. "She'll be fine, Spud," he promised. "Did you work out that last problem?"

The child nodded, closing her books and putting her papers in a neat stack. It was a trait she'd probably gotten from Glory, Jesse reflected, since he tended to leave things scattered about.

"So what do you want to do?"

Liza's face brightened. "Let's get the Christmas stuff down from the attic. That way, we'll be all ready to decorate when we get the tree."

Jesse sighed dramatically, but he liked the idea as well as Liza did. He was looking forward to

Christmas this year, though he'd spent the last ten dreading it. "Okay," he said, shaking his finger. "But it's a school night and you're not staying up till all hours."

She grinned. "Don't worry, Uncle Jesse. I'll mind real good."

They brought the nativity scene down first; it had been one of Jesse's mother's most valued possessions, and he carried it carefully. The porcelain figures had been handcrafted in Italy before he was born, but he and Gresham had built the stable out in the carriage house one year, as a surprise.

After the crèche had been set in its place of honor, on the raised hearth of the living-room fireplace, the figures arranged just so, Jesse and Liza went back to the attic for the boxes and boxes of delicate ornaments and lights that always graced the tree.

Jesse was actually humming a Christmas carol as he sat in the middle of the living-room floor, a fire blazing on the hearth, untangling strings of lights. Liza had hooked them all together and plugged them in, and he suddenly found himself surrounded by bright knobs of color.

He laughed. "You're no help, at all."

Liza came and sat beside him, amid the twinkling tangle, and laid her head against his shoulder. Her statement caught him unaware, even though he should have been on the alert after that conversation they'd had earlier. "I think my real dad and mom might live around here."

We got trouble, Jesse thought, *right here in Pearl River. And it starts with a capital G.* "Why do you say that?" he asked, still working with the twisted strings of rubber-coated wire.

"It's just a feeling," Liza answered. But then she pinioned him with those eyes of hers and asked him straight out, "Do you know who my dad is, Uncle Jesse?"

He answered hoarsely, without knowing why he did it. He was sure of only one thing: that lying to this kid was impossible. "Yes, Button. I know."

"Who is he?"

Jesse drew a deep breath, exhaled, and set the lights aside to draw Liza gently onto his lap. She gazed into his face with total trust.

"He's me," he said raggedly, holding her tighter.

She didn't seem shocked. In fact, she didn't even seem surprised. "How come you gave me to Daddy and Mommy?"

"I didn't, exactly." Jesse tucked her head under his chin. "But it worked out okay, didn't it? I mean, your daddy and mommy really loved you, and they took good care of you."

Liza twisted in his lap, so she could look him directly in the eye again. "But they're gone," she reasoned. "If you're my dad, you know who my mother is. Tell me, Uncle Jesse—please."

Jesse shook his head. He'd had all the emotional strain he could handle for right then, and besides, he needed time to think before he gave Glory a permanent place in Liza's life. She swore she'd changed, but Glory had a habit of disappearing just when somebody started loving her with everything they had. "I can't do that, sweetheart. At least not tonight. For right now, I'm going to ask you to trust me and to believe that I'll tell you when the time is right."

She reached up to kiss his cheek, then settled her head under his chin again. "I love you, Jesse," she said, and for a moment the scattered tree lights blended before Jesse's eyes, making a collage of Christmas colors.

"I love you, too, kid," he answered gruffly.

8

Liza arrived at the bank about five minutes before closing time and waited quietly in one of the
chairs in Glory's office. The child seemed distracted, and Glory was troubled by that.

"Is something wrong?" she asked, as she put on
her coat and reached for her purse.

Liza's small shoulders moved in a shrug.
"Sometimes I wish I could be Nancy Drew and go
around solving mysteries."

Glory put a hand on Liza's back and ushered her
through the office door. "What mysteries would
you solve?"

The little girl looked up with an expression of
despairing resignation. "I'd find out who my real
mom is, and ask her why she didn't want me."

A painful lump formed in Glory's throat, but she
made herself smile in spite of it. "I'll bet she
wanted you very, very much," she said.

Liza shrugged again, and the two of them hurried out to Glory's car. Glory turned on the engine and shivered as she waited for the heater to kick in.

At home, Glory made cocoa for Liza and a *latte* for herself. The apartment was warm; evidently the temperamental radiators were having a good day. Since Glory had spent the evening before putting things away, the place looked relatively tidy.

"You should put your Christmas tree right here," Liza announced, standing by the bay windows that overlooked the street. She turned in a circle, with her arms stretched wide, as though clearing a space in the cosmos.

"I thought I would," Glory agreed, setting the cocoa and *latte* down on the coffee table in front of her pale rose couch.

"When are you doing to put it up?" Liza inquired.

"This weekend, I hope. I'll probably get one while we're out tree hunting on Saturday."

Liza's smile was a little forlorn as she came to sit in Glory's mauve wing chair and reached for her cocoa. It was plain she was trying to work up her courage to say something, and when she did, the words practically stopped Glory's heart. "If a person loses one daddy, and then they get another one, can the second one die, too?"

She set her *latte* on the coffee table so it wouldn't spill over onto the rug. Obviously, Jesse had told Liza who he was, but what had he said about her biological mother? Damn it, he might have warned her! She drew a deep breath and forcibly controlled herself! "Honey, anybody can die, and most of the time we don't know when it's going to happen." She paused, praying silently for the right words. "The thing is, you can't plan your life to avoid pain. You can't say, 'I'm not going to love this person, because if I do, I might get hurt somewhere down the road.'"

Unexpectedly, Liza began to cry. She put her cocoa down, crossed the distance between their chairs and scrambled into Glory's lap, sobbing.

Glory held her child, her own eyes blurred with tears. "It's okay, darling. You go right ahead and cry."

"Uncle Jesse is a cop!" wailed the little girl. "He could get shot by a bad guy, or his car might go off the road when he's chasing somebody—"

Glory kissed Liza's temple. "He could also live to be a very old man, honey, like his grandfather."

After a while, Liza began to settle down. "I g-guess you'd better measure me for my costume," she said, sniffling. "I have to go and practice for the pageant tonight, and Aunt Ilene will be here to pick me up after she closes the store."

With a nod, Glory set her daughter on her feet and went to get her sewing basket. She measured Liza according to the mimeographed directions.

It was Jesse who came by to pick the child up a few minutes later, not Ilene. He sent Liza to wait in the car and lingered outside Glory's door, his hands in his coat pockets, his expression guarded and remote.

"You told her," Glory said, standing there in the doorway. She knew he wouldn't come in even if she invited him.

Jesse sighed. "Yeah. I told her part of it." He paused for a moment before dropping the bomb that blew Glory's tentative dreams to bits. "Liza's been through more at nine than most people endure in a lifetime," he said. "I want you to stay away from her until everybody gets their emotional balance back."

For a moment, Glory held on to the hope that she hadn't heard him right. "Stay away?" she echoed in a small voice.

"I don't want her to get attached to you, Glory, only to be hurt later when you decide small towns and kids aren't 'you' and move on."

There was, unfortunately, no doubting what he'd meant that time. "I won't let you do this, Jesse—I love that child as much as you do."

His response was a quietly furious, "You can talk about love, but it takes a hell of a lot more than that to raise a kid. You've got to be able to stick out the tough times, and I don't think you know how to do that."

He turned then, and started to walk away. Glory started to call him back, then stopped herself. Jesse had obviously made up his mind and, for now, there would be no reasoning with him.

She closed the door quietly behind him, spread the white synthetic taffeta for Liza's costume out on the kitchen table and tried to focus her tear-filled eyes on the printed instructions. She worked straight through dinner and by ten o'clock she had the outfit finished, right down to the tinsel halo and gauze wings trimmed with silver garland.

The next morning Glory dressed and went to work as usual, dropping off Liza's costume at Ilene's bookstore without saying more than a muttered, "Good morning." Reaching the bank, she got out Pearl River's thin phone book and looked under "attorneys" for the name of a lawyer.

There were only two in town, and the first one, Glory recalled, had been one of Jesse's closest friends since kindergarten. She called the second, a man named Brock Haywood, and made an appointment.

He agreed to see her during her lunch hour.

* * *

On Saturday morning, Glory bought a tree from the straggly group displayed in front of the supermarket. One of the bag boys tied it to the roof of her car, and she headed straight home.

Whatever Christmas spirit she'd mustered was gone—she was only putting up the tree for appearance's sake. Delphine and Harold would be worried if she didn't do something to observe the holiday.

She was putting lights on the tree, having set it in its stand in front of the bay windows in her living room, when Jill pulled up. Glory was relieved to see her friend, but she also felt a desire to hide.

Of course she couldn't since Jill had seen her.

"I thought you were going tree-hunting with Jesse and Liza," Glory's friend commented as she divested herself of her coat, hat and gloves. "I wouldn't have stopped, if I hadn't caught a glimpse of you through the window as I was driving by."

Glory repeated a silent litany of reasons why she must not burst into tears and then said, in an awkward attempt to change the subject, "Weren't you supposed to be skiing this weekend with that new boyfriend of yours?"

Jill rolled her eyes. "He turned out to be another creep." She plopped herself down in one of Glory's chairs. "I swear, if I ever do find a man I like they'll probably feature him on 'Unsolved Mysteries' as an ax murderer.''

Glory laughed, despite the pain of her own situation. "How about some hot cider, or a *latte*?"

"A *latte*? You sophisticated creature! I'll have one of those."

The process of brewing two of the concoctions gave Glory time to pull herself together. It was inevitable, after all, that Jill would ask again why she wasn't spending the day with Jesse and Liza as planned.

She sprang the question as soon as Glory returned with the two steaming cups and sat down on the sofa. "What happened between you and Jesse?"

Glory sighed. She'd never told Jill the whole truth, but it spilled out of her now, all of it. She related how the judge had forced her to leave town, how she'd come back and discovered that the daughter she'd given up had been adopted by Gresham and Sandy, how Jesse had ordered her to stay away from Liza for the time being.

"And you're letting him get away with it?" Jill demanded, her face a study in disbelief.

"No," Glory answered, shaking her head. "I've filed a suit for visitation rights." She glanced at her watch and sighed again. "Jesse should be getting the papers soon."

Jill put down her cup and covered her ears with both hands, as if expecting an explosion. After a moment, she grinned shakily and dropped them to her lap. "This ought to give tonight's Christmas pageant a high degree of dramatic tension. You are coming, aren't you?"

Glory nodded. "Nothing could keep me away."

"Good for you," Jill answered resolutely. That was easy for her to say, Glory thought. She wasn't playing with emotional dynamite.

"Jesse Bainbridge?"

Jesse stopped in the hallway of Pearl River's tiny courthouse, frowning at the old man who stood before him. "You know who I am, Harry," he said. "I used to deliver your newspapers."

Harry flushed. "I'm sorry, Jesse," he said. And then he held out a folded document.

Jesse muttered a curse and accepted the papers without asking for a further explanation. He knew a summons when he saw one, and nobody needed to tell him who was behind it.

Delphine and Harold arrived at Glory's apartment at six o'clock sharp, bringing a potted red poinsettia. While Delphine set the plant on the coffee table, Harold sniffed the air and smiled appreciatively.

"Something sure smells good," he boomed in his big voice. "I'll bet you're as good a cook as your mother." He put an arm around Delphine's slender shoulders and squeezed.

Glory made an effort at a smile. "It's my specialty, Spanish rice," she replied.

Harold said he was looking forward to supper and sat down in one of the living-room chairs to watch the news on TV. Delphine joined Glory in the kitchen.

"You look like hell warmed over," she told her daughter bluntly. "What's happened?"

Glory made a major enterprise of taking the casserole dish from the oven and getting the salad out of the fridge. "Thanks for the poinsettia, Mama," she said, hoping to deflect the conversation. "It's lovely."

"Glory."

She sighed and faced her mother squarely, setting the Spanish rice on a trivet on the counter. "Jesse declared war a few days ago, and I fired back."

"What do you mean, Jesse declared war?"

"He told Liza that he's her father. Then he told *me* to stay away from her until further notice. So I saw a lawyer and filed for visitation rights."

Delphine's normally pink cheeks went white for a moment. "Uh-oh. What was Jesse's response to that?"

"I don't know yet," Glory said. "He probably didn't get the papers until this afternoon."

Delphine gave a deep sigh, then put her arms around Glory and hugged her tightly. "Well, what's done is done. Harold and I will stick by you, of course."

Glory returned her mother's embrace before stepping back. "I'm sorry this had to happen now, Mama, right before your wedding and everything."

Delphine and Harold were to be married on New Year's Eve, in a candlelight service at the First Lutheran Church. "You have enough to worry about without fretting over that," the older woman said. "We'll all just have to take this one step at a time."

"You're on my side?" Glory asked, surprised, as, still wearing oven mitts, she picked up the casserole dish to carry it to the table in the dining area. Delphine followed with the salad.

"Good heavens, sweetheart, did you expect me to take Jesse's part? I'm *your* mother."

"I know you like Jesse."

Delphine kissed Glory's cheek. "Maybe so, but I *love* you."

After that, she and Delphine and Harold had a quiet dinner amid the twinkling sparkles cast by the tree. As soon as they'd cleared away the dishes, it was time to leave for the Christmas pageant.

"When you get home tonight, after seeing Liza again," Glory said to her mother, when she was settled in the backseat of Harold's car, "I want you to take a good look at that old picture of your grandmother Bridget."

Delphine nodded, but her smile was tempered with sadness, and she was quiet as they all drove to the church.

The requisite snow was falling as they left the car and followed the crowd up the steps and into the building. In the sanctuary, fragrant garlands of evergreen decorated the altar railings, and someone had constructed a remarkably authentic stable on the dais, complete with straw. There were candles waiting on the pews, and each person took one before sitting down.

Glory quickly scanned the crowd for Jesse and was relieved not to see him. Maybe, she thought in a spate of wild optimism, he was somewhere battling crime and wouldn't be able to attend the pageant, at all.

He came in about one second after she'd formulated the idea and took a place in the pew directly in front of hers, turning to give her a challenging stare.

Harold, who suspected nothing, thrust out his hand and said, "Hello, Jesse. How's the lawman business these days?"

Jesse's face thawed visibly as he shook Harold's hand. "Unfortunately, it's thriving." He looked at Delphine and gave her a roguish wink. "By the way, Harold, congratulations on marrying the prettiest girl in town."

His friendliness to Harold and Delphine, which clearly shut her out, was almost as difficult for Glory to cope with as the cold anger he bore toward her. It was a tremendous relief to her when the organist started the prelude and everyone sat down.

Candles were lit, and the lights turned down, and the pastor delivered a short sermon on the significance of the season. Glory tried to concentrate on the real meaning of Christmas, but all she could do was stare at the back of Jesse's head and ache because even after all these years they couldn't be civil to each other.

Presently the pastor finished speaking, and the pageant began. Mary and Joseph came up the center aisle to a cardboard door set up at one side of the dais, and Joseph knocked, causing it to waver dangerously.

The innkeeper opened it and, with audible prompting from Jill, who was sitting in the front pew, informed the weary couple that there was no room at the inn. They could, however, sleep in the stable if they wanted to.

Mary and Joseph trekked wearily over to the makeshift barn. They knelt in the straw, as if to pray, and there was a moment of dramatic import before Jill rushed up and put a baby doll in the manger.

Meanwhile, shepherds came up the aisle in burlap robes, with bath towels on their heads and sandals on their feet, and angels fluttered in through the doorway to the pastor's study. Glory's heart surged into her throat as she watched Liza take her place with the others, resplendent in her costume.

There were songs and Bible verses, but Glory had eyes and ears only for her daughter. Like Mary, she pondered the miracle of birth in her heart.

All too quickly, the evening ended. As the players filed down the aisle to collect their reward of cookies and hot cider in the church fellowship hall, Liza's eyes linked with Glory's, and Glory felt a stab at the sorrow she saw in her child's gaze.

Obviously Jesse had announced his decision to keep Glory and Liza apart. An anger entirely unsuited to her surroundings welled up inside Glory, and she rushed out of the sanctuary, through the narthex, and outside into the biting cold. There she stood gripping the stair railing, her eyes burning with furious tears.

She sensed Jesse's presence a moment before he came to stand on the step beside her.

"Glory—"

She crammed her hands into her coat pockets so she wouldn't start pounding at his chest in an hysterical rage. "Did you think I wouldn't fight back, Jesse?" she whispered. "Did you think I'd let you take Liza away from me, like your grandfather did?"

"Glory, listen to me."

"No, I won't listen to you!" Glory blurted out, moving the rest of the way down the steps. "I've heard it all, Jesse. You say you're afraid I'll make Liza love me and then desert her, but the real truth is you want to punish me for hurting *you*! You're not thinking about her, you're thinking about yourself!"

Although most people had gone downstairs to share in the celebration and the refreshments, there were a few souls trailing out to go home. Both Glory and Jesse lapsed into a stiff silence until they were alone again.

Then he took her arm and hustled her a little way down the street. "Maybe I am thinking about myself—after all, I'm the one who's had the most experience with your methods—but you're not operating out of pure altruism yourself, lady. You want to soothe your conscience, and you're not going to use Liza to do it!''

"She'll guess, Jesse," Glory said evenly, having made a great effort at keeping her temper. "It doesn't take a rocket scientist to count backwards ten years and look at the pictures in a high-school yearbook!"

"I'll handle that when it happens. Right now, I want you to leave her alone."

Before Glory could reply, she saw an angel with pigtails standing on the church steps and gazing wistfully in their direction. Glory ached with everything in her to gather the child into her arms and tell her that she loved her, that giving her up was the single greatest regret of her life. "Let's call a cease-fire for now, Jesse," she said with a sigh. "An angel has just stepped into range."

Jesse turned and saw Liza there and instantly he was in motion. "You were fantastic!" he told his daughter, scooping her into his arms and starting up the church steps. "Let's go get some of that cider before it's all gone."

Over Jesse's shoulder, Liza stared forlornly back at Glory and wiggled her fingers in farewell.

Struggling to regain her equilibrium, Glory waited on the steps until Delphine and Harold came out a few minutes later. Maybe Jesse was right, she thought miserably, as her mother and future step-father drove her home. Maybe she was just think-ing of herself, and it would be better if she moved on and started a new life somewhere else.

After saying good-night to Delphine and Har-old, Glory went into her apartment and flipped on the Christmas-tree lights, leaving the rest of the living room dark. Then she sank down onto the couch, still wearing her coat and gloves, and mur-mured, "Oh, Dylan, what should I do—stay or go?"

She supposed talking to her dead brother—a foible that seemed excusable when she was stand-ing beside his grave—meant she'd finally gone around the bend in the river and would never be able to paddle back, but she didn't care.

The radiators clanged, but Glory knew that wasn't a message from the other side. It just meant the landlord was too cheap to put in a modern heating system. With a sigh she took off her coat and gloves, kicked away her boots and flipped on the television set.

Glory watched one program and then another and then another, and if her life had depended on it she couldn't have said what any of the shows was about. Awakening to find herself hunched up on the couch, cold and achy, she rose, switched off the TV and the tree lights and went to bed.

Tomorrow was another day, and the war between her and Jesse would undoubtedly continue. She'd need her strength.

In the morning, Glory went through her usual routine of showering, eating breakfast, putting on her makeup, blow drying her hair and getting dressed. She felt like a wooden mannequin, caused by some unseen magician to move and function but not quite brought to life.

Since the bank didn't open until ten, and Glory reported to work at nine, she used her key to let herself in. The two tellers smiled and said "Good morning" in chorus, and Glory, still the mannequin, responded as if she'd been programmed.

She'd no more than put away her purse and gotten out her appointment book for the day when Shelby, one of the secretaries, came in with coffee. She was a pretty dark-eyed girl with long chocolate-brown hair.

"Someone evidently came by to see you either last night or this morning," Shelby said with a smile, producing an envelope and setting it on Glory's desk, along with the coffee. "I found this in the night depository."

A feeling of dread clenched Glory's heart and stomach as she picked up the envelope. Her name was written across the front in teetering cursive letters. "Thank you," she said distractedly, wanting to be alone.

Shelby left, and Glory opened the envelope and took out the folded page of notebook paper inside.

Dear Glory, the same childish hand had written, and Glory groped blindly for the telephone receiver as she read on.

Liza stood uncertainly beside the railroad track, holding her Uncle Jesse's high-school yearbook under one arm and her piggy bank under the other. When the train stopped—as yet, there was no sign of it—Liza meant to climb into one of the freight cars just like she'd seen a girl do in the movies once.

Her feet were cold, even though she had two pairs of socks inside her boots. She'd worn jeans and a flannel shirt and thermal underwear so she wouldn't get sick and die, like Beth in *Little Women*.

She sniffled. She probably shouldn't have climbed up on the concrete edge that protected the flower bed at the bank and dropped that stupid note into the night-deposit box, because Glory would most likely call Uncle Jesse as soon as she read it.

Glory. Awkwardly, Liza set the piggy bank and the yearbook down in the snow and hugged herself. If Glory didn't want to be her mommy, it was all right. Liza didn't want to be Glory's daughter, either.

Much.

In the distance the train whistle hooted, and Liza drew in her breath. She was afraid the tears would freeze in her eyelashes if she cried, and she *really* wanted to cry.

She supposed she'd known Glory was somebody special from the first time she'd met her. Last night, lying in bed, all wide awake from the excitement of the Christmas pageant, the whole thing had come to Liza in a shattering flash. The words she'd heard Glory say on the sidewalk in front of the church had come back to her, their meaning crystal-clear.

She'll guess, Jesse. It doesn't take a rocket scientist to count backwards ten years and look at the pictures in a high-school yearbook!

Uncle Jesse was her father, he'd admitted it himself. And he and Glory had been in love ten years before, and Liza was nine years old. It took nine months for a baby to grow inside a woman's stomach, according to a special she and Aunt Ilene had watched on PBS. Besides that, Aunt Ilene had told her just the other day that Uncle Jesse was always mad at Glory because he'd loved her very much once upon a time and she'd gone away.

Liza wiped her nose with a mittened hand. If she could have had any woman in the world for a mommy, besides the one she'd lost in the plane crash, of course, she would have picked Glory Parsons. That made the thought that Glory hadn't wanted her, that she'd gone off and left her all alone in some hospital right after she was *born*, for pity's sake, impossible for Liza to accept.

She'd decided to go away somewhere and raise herself. Even the fact that it was almost Christmas and she probably would have gotten a Nintendo from Uncle Jesse couldn't make her stay.

The train chugged around a corner, coming out of the snowy trees, making a great clatter as it approached. Liza had seen it stop in just this place about ten million times, so she stooped and picked up the yearbook and the piggy bank and prepared to jump on board.

The whistle shrieked a greeting, and Liza waited patiently, hoping that raising herself wouldn't cost more than $15.87.

"Jesse!" Glory gasped the moment the sheriff of Pearl River County came on the line. "Liza's run away! She left a note in the night depository—oh, God, Jesse, *do something*!"

His voice was surprisingly calm. "Glory, take a deep breath and get a grip on yourself. Did she say where she was going?"

"No," Glory burst out, half sick with panic.

"Read me the note," Jesse said evenly.

Glory began, the lined notebook paper crackling in her hand because she was trembling so hard.

Dear Glory,
If you don't want me, that's okay, because I don't want you, either. You left me at the hospital. The reason I can't stay is, I don't want you and Uncle Jesse to fight about me anymore. And I don't want to see you in the bank and know you didn't like me enough to keep me. I know Uncle Jesse and Aunt Ilene will miss me a whole lot, and I would have got a bunch of presents at Christmas. I guess they can take back whatever stuff they bought and get a refund.

Love, Liza

"Listen to me," Jesse said, his voice stern. "We're going to find her. I'll send a deputy to the bus station and we'll cover all the highways leading out of town. *Liza will be all right,* Glory."

"Like Dylan was all right?" Glory cried. "Like Sandy and Gresham—"

"Stop it, Glory. I don't have time for this."

"Come and get me, Jesse. I want to go with you."

Jesse gave in, but reluctantly. "I'll be there in five minutes. If you're not waiting on the sidewalk, I won't even slow down, let alone stop and twiddle my thumbs until you come out of the bank. Is that clear?"

Glory was already out of her chair and groping for her purse. "It's clear, Jesse. I promise it's clear."

He hung up with a crash, and Glory ran to tell Mr. Baker there was an emergency in the family, but she didn't explain the details. He very kindly excused her to go and take care of it, calling after her that he hoped everything would work out all right.

Jesse's patrol car appeared an instant after she stepped out of the bank and, as good as his word, he just barely stopped at all. The tires were spinning again before Glory had managed to close her door or fasten the seat belt.

"I hope you're satisfied," Jesse rasped, just before he reached for the microphone to radio the men he'd dispatched to different parts of town.

Glory bit into her lower lip and said nothing. If anything had happened to Liza, she was never going to forgive herself.

9

"This is all my fault," Glory fretted as she and Jesse began the search for their runaway daughter. "If I hadn't come back here—"

Jesse's jawline hardened for a moment, but then he reached out and touched Glory's knee. "Take it easy," he told her. "Liza's nine years old—she couldn't have gotten far."

Glory didn't find it at all comforting to realize that Jesse was taking the road that led to the small park down by the river. The water would be frigid at this time of year, even frozen over in places, and Glory's whole being seemed to clench in terror as she prayed Liza hadn't gone there.

"W-why the river?" she managed to ask, when Jesse brought the patrol car to a stop in the small, freshly plowed parking area that overlooked an array of snow-mounded picnic tables and barbecue pits.

"We've had some happy times here," Jesse said in a hoarse, distant voice. "Watch out that you don't break your neck in those damn high heels."

Only then did Glory realize that she wasn't suitably dressed for a search in her gray Ultrasuede suit, ruffly blouse and charcoal eel-skin heels. She was out of the car as fast as Jesse was, but keeping pace with him immediately proved impossible.

He started down the pristine slope toward the picnic area, his strides long, his plain boots perfectly suited to the task. Cupping his hands to his mouth, he yelled, "Liza!"

Glory picked her way along behind him, moving as fast as she could, her eyes scanning the river, with its shards of sun-glittered ice. *Please God,* she prayed, *don't let her be in that water.*

Jesse gave the landscape around them what Glory perceived to be a cursory examination, then announced, his breath white in the crisp air, "She isn't here."

"How do you know?" Glory demanded. Even though she'd just prayed that Liza hadn't come near the river, she wanted to leave no stone unturned.

With a sweeping gesture of one arm, Jesse took in the whole park. "No tracks in the snow. Nobody's been down here in the last few days except us." His brown eyes ran over Glory's inadequate clothing with a sort of tolerant contempt. Then, without a word of warning, he strode over to her, lifted her up into his arms, and started carrying her toward the parking lot. "You're heavier than you look," he commented.

Glory tried to ignore what being held so close to Jesse did to her, even under such uncertain circumstances. If she'd known Liza was safe and warm somewhere, Glory would have wanted him to make love to her. "Thanks," she retorted.

Reaching the parking lot, Jesse set Glory back on her feet with an exaggerated sigh of relief. Moments later, he was in the front seat of his car, the microphone to his radio in one hand.

Glory heard the blunt, static-ridden answers to his questions as she snapped her seat belt in place, but she couldn't make sense of what was being said.

"They didn't find her at the bus station," he said, staring out at the river as he put the microphone back in place, "and there's no sign of her along any of the roads leading out of town."

Panic rose around Glory like invisible floodwaters, threatening to drown her, but Jesse offered her hope as he started the car and shifted into reverse.

"That probably means she's still somewhere in Pearl River," he said.

Shivering with cold and fear, Glory hugged herself. "Maybe she went to your house, Jesse. There are a lot of outbuildings there, if I remember correctly, and she probably has happy memories of the place.''

''It's worth checking out,'' Jesse agreed. And then he headed back to the main highway.

It took a full forty-five minutes to search every nook and cranny in the Bainbridge mansion, and there was no sign of Liza anywhere between the wine cellar and the attic. The stables, carriage house, storage sheds and the guest house were all empty, too.

In the mansion's huge kitchen, Jesse made instant coffee for Glory, lacing it generously with brandy, and then grabbed at the wall phone and punched out a number. Glory knew without being told that he was calling his office, hoping against hope that there would be some word.

She thought she'd faint with relief when, after barking a greeting, Jesse grinned. ''Liza's been found,'' he said to Glory. ''She went to the diner after she missed her train, and she's okay.''

Glory swayed against the counter and took a restorative sip of her coffee. *Thank you, God,* she thought, closing her eyes. *Thank you, thank you, thank you!*

After a few more words, none of which Glory was able to grasp, Jesse hung up the receiver with a triumphant crash.

Glory started to set her coffee aside, but Jesse stopped her with a crisp, "Drink it down. You're white as hell." Then he took her arm and led her to the bench beside the big trestle table.

Knowing Jesse wouldn't take her to her daughter until she'd done what he said, Glory sat down on the bench and drank her spiked coffee as fast as she could swallow it. Then they returned to Jesse's squad car and started toward town.

Instead of heading toward the diner, Jesse took the first right turn after they crossed the city limits and brought the squad car to a stop in front of Dr. Cupples's humble office. It was a small blue house with white shutters, and the doctor's shingle hung from the scrollwork above the porch.

Glory hadn't been near the place since that day a decade before, when she'd learned she was pregnant with Jesse's baby. Despite the unhappy memories, she was right behind Jesse as he strode up the walk.

"I thought you said Liza is all right!" she cried breathlessly, when he reached the porch and wrenched open the front door.

"Johnson brought her here, just to make sure," Jesse answered shortly. And then he was looming over the receptionist's desk, demanding, "Where's my daughter?"

"Right in there," the middle-aged woman replied, pointing toward a doorway, not in the least intimidated by the sheriff's manner.

As quickly as Glory moved, Jesse was through the doorway first.

Liza sat on the end of an examining table, wrapped in an oversized, old-fashioned felt bathrobe with Indian designs on it, sipping hot cocoa. Her eyes went wide when she saw Jesse.

He shook his finger at her. "You're just lucky I'm too glad to see you to tan your hide!" he told the child furiously.

Liza looked from Jesse's face to Glory's, then sighed like a ninety-year-old woman. "I'm sorry," she said, her little shoulders stooped.

Glory spoke far more gently than Jesse had. "Why did you do it?" she asked. Even though she was sure she knew, she still hoped she'd been wrong. "Why did you run away?"

Liza's gaze was level. "Because you didn't want me. I would probably be halfway to California by now, if that darned train had just stopped."

Just then Dr. Cupples appeared in another doorway. He was an old man now, with white hair and kindly blue eyes. "Hello, Jesse," he said. Then hesitantly he added a greeting for Glory. "Ms. Parsons. I wonder if I could speak with the two of you in my office."

Jesse nodded shortly, and his brown eyes were hot as they swung back to his daughter. "I still haven't decided against spanking you," he warned, "so don't you dare move!"

Glory, for her part, was swamped with memories as she preceded Jesse into the doctor's small office. Here, the physician had given her happy news that was to have tragic, far-reaching results. She felt weak as she sank into one of the chairs facing Dr. Cupples's desk.

Jesse took the other, lifting one booted foot to rest on the opposite knee.

The doctor carefully closed the office door, then went behind his desk to sink into his swivel chair with a weary sigh. He pressed a button on his telephone and said, "Doris, will you please hold my calls for a few minutes?"

Jesse shifted uncomfortably in his chair, then leaned forward, his brows drawn together in a frown. "What's this all about?"

The old man sat back, making a steeple of his fingers beneath his double chin. "I have a confession to make, and it's not an easy thing to do, Jesse Bainbridge, so I'll thank you to keep your pants on until I get it said!"

Still glowering, Jesse subsided a little, settling back in his chair. Glory, meanwhile was perched on the edge of hers, sensing that Dr. Cupples was about to make an important announcement.

"After you came to see me that day ten years ago, Glory," he said with resignation, "I betrayed your trust—and my own vows as a physician—to call my friend Seth Bainbridge and tell him you were expecting a baby, and that Jesse was the father."

Glory wasn't surprised; she'd deduced that long ago. But Jesse straightened in his chair, poised like a rocket about to shoot off the launchpad.

"What?" he rasped.

"I thought I was doing a friend a favor. Now, of course, I wish I'd just stayed out of the whole thing. That little girl out there might have been a whole lot happier if I had." Dr. Cupples sighed and leaned forward, bracing his forearms against his cluttered desk. "The judge thought it was important for you to go to college and marry well, Jesse, so he paid Ms. Parsons to leave town."

Jesse shot a lethal look in Glory's direction. "Don't blame yourself too much, Doc," he rasped. "The plan wouldn't have worked if Glory hadn't been so damn willing to be bought off!"

Glory would have liked to think Jesse didn't mean what he was saying, that he was just reacting to the unavoidable stress of losing a child and finding her again, but she knew he meant every word.

And she was too crippled with hurt and regret to defend herself.

"Glory was eighteen," Doc Cupples pointed out kindly. "A fatherless girl, with nobody to take her side." His blue eyes shifted to Glory's face. "You have no idea how sorry I am for my interference, my dear, or how much I wish I'd done something to help you."

Jesse thrust himself out of his chair and stormed out of the office, and Glory followed him, after one apologetic look at the doctor.

In the examination room, Jesse scooped Liza up in his arms, borrowed bathrobe, and all, and held her tightly against his chest. His gaze punctured Glory's spirit like a lance. "You and your lawyer wanted a fight," he breathed. "Well, lady, you've got one!"

Before Glory could work through the wall of pain that surrounded her and respond, Jesse strode out, carrying Liza with him.

Dr. Cupples laid one hand on Glory's shoulder. "Jesse's a good man," he said quietly, "even if he is hot-tempered. He'll come to his senses if you just give him a day or two."

Glory felt broken and bruised inside. She nodded distractedly and went out.

Walking to her mother's diner, she heard Liza's words over and over in her mind...*you didn't want me*....

When Delphine saw her daughter, she was visibly horrified. Stepping back to admit Glory to the little apartment over the diner, she said, "Glory, sweetheart, what's happened? I thought you'd be happy, finding Liza safe—"

Glory sank into a chair and kicked off her eelskin shoes. They were completely ruined, but she didn't give a damn. "You were right," she said brokenly. "You were right."

Delphine bent to unbutton Glory's coat, as she might have done when her daughter was a child, and pushed it back off her shoulders. Then she took the crocheted afghan from the sofa and draped it tenderly around Glory's legs. "There, now," she whispered soothingly. "What was I so right about?"

"I shouldn't have come here," Glory fretted in utter despair. "All I did was mix Liza up. She ran away because she thought I didn't want her. And, Mama, she could have been hurt or even killed. Someone awful might have picked her up—"

"Hush!" Delphine interrupted with affectionate harshness. "The child is safe and sound, Glory—that's all that matters." She moved toward the kitchen to brew the inevitable cup of tea, always part of her solution to any heartbreak. "You were right about one thing," she said cheerfully. "That little girl is the spitting image of Bridget McVerdy!"

Glory began to cry softly. Liza might have been saved all this trauma if Glory had just kept her promise to the judge and stayed away from Pearl River. But no, she'd had to come here and blow the lid off everything. Now Liza would not only grieve for Sandy and Gresham, she would suffer with the knowledge that her birth parents had failed her.

When Delphine returned with tea, a little plate of colorful Christmas cookies and a packet of tissue, Glory was slightly calmer. She dried her eyes, no doubt smearing her makeup all over her face, and then blew her nose. When that process was completed, she accepted one cookie and the strong, fragrant tea.

"There is one obvious solution to all this, you know," Delphine said gently, sitting down on the sofa facing Glory and folding her hands.

"What?" Glory sniffled, taking a disconsolate bite out of an angel's wing.

"You and Jesse could get married. Then the two of you could go about making a life for yourselves and your daughter."

Glory shook her head. "I'll admit it, Mama— I'm just crazy enough that I'm as much in love with

Jesse as I ever was. I g-guess I'm one of those women who loves pain. But there's no hope for us. Jesse's furious with me—he can't see past the fact that I took money from the judge when I left Pearl River. I hurt him far more deeply than I ever dreamed I could, and he's never going to forgive me.''

"Why don't you decide that after you've gone to him and told him the truth, Glory—that you love him desperately?"

Glory imagined the scenario and shrank from the accusations she knew she would see burning in Jesse's eyes. "I can't."

"It would seem you're not all that crazy about pain, after all," Delphine observed with a wry twist to her mouth. She reached for a reindeer cookie and bit off its antlers.

Glory sighed. "You know, Mama, I wish I were more like you. You've had lots of heartache in your life, but it never broke you. You were brave. You just kept putting one foot in front of the other and, lo and behold, here you are with a business of your own and a man who adores you."

"Do you think I never ran away from a problem?" Delphine asked, raising her eyebrows. "If you do, you don't have a very good memory. When we came here to Pearl River, you and Dylan and I, we were on the run from a very bad situation."

"But you started over. You made the best of things. What would you do if you were me?"

"Knowing what I know now? I'd stand toe to toe with Jesse Bainbridge and tell him I loved him. Then I'd work at my job and I'd find a way to build some kind of relationship with Liza."

Glory set her teacup aside. She wasn't as courageous as her mother; she couldn't endure Jesse's hatred, or the knowledge that she'd done her own child more harm than good. No, the best thing to do would be to go away.

Eventually Liza's wounds would heal over and so, hopefully, would her own.

She set the afghan aside and rose shakily to her feet. "I'd better go home," she said. "I have things to do."

"I'll drive you there," Delphine told her, standing and going to the closet for her own coat.

"That won't be necessary, Mama," Glory protested woodenly. "My car's at the bank."

"You're in no shape to walk even that far," Delphine insisted. "And you've ruined your shoes. I doubt they'll even stay on your feet."

Sure enough, the high heels were destined for the rubbish bin. Glory accepted a pair of her mother's slippers, since any of her shoes would have been too small, and obediently followed her downstairs to Delphine's little silver car.

Delphine didn't take Glory to the bank parking lot, she took her directly to her apartment. There, she undressed her like a child, put her into a warm flannel nightgown, turned up the heat, and tucked her into bed. Then Delphine brought her a cup of hot lemon juice mixed with water and honey and two aspirin tablets.

Glory dutifully took the aspirin and sipped the lemon concoction. "I'm not sick," she protested.

"You will be, if someone doesn't take care of you," Delphine responded firmly. And then she left the room, and Glory heard her talking on the telephone, telling Harold she was spending the night at her daughter's apartment.

When Glory had finished her drink, she settled down into the covers and closed her eyes. She'd just rest for a few minutes, then she'd get up and telephone her attorney, and Mr. Baker at the bank.

When she awakened, she was instantly aware that hours had passed. Delphine was humming along with Christmas carols on the radio, and something smelled heavenly.

Glory got out of bed and, after a short visit to the bathroom, ventured into the kitchen. The tree was lit, belying the fact that suffering existed anywhere in the world.

Pulling back a chair at the table, Glory sat down. "Hi," she said.

Delphine kissed her forehead, and once again Glory thought how much she'd missed having someone to fuss over her when things were going wrong. "Hi, sweetie. I cooked your favorite for supper—spaghetti and meatballs."

Glory sighed. "That was a good trick, since I didn't have anything in the cupboards or the fridge—I was planning on going shopping tonight after work."

Back at the stove, Delphine was stirring the savory sauce she and she alone could make. Her slender shoulders moved in a pretty shrug. "Harold stopped by the supermarket for me."

"You should have invited him to stay for supper," Glory said, feeling guilty. Here she was, a grown woman, getting in the way of her mother's romance.

"I did," Delphine answered. "He said we needed this time together without him hanging around, getting in the way. Those were his words, by the way, not mine."

Glory propped her chin in one hand. "He's a great guy," she said. "I think if I didn't love you so much, I'd be jealous."

Delphine smiled. "You might find that Jesse is a 'great guy,' if you'd just wade through all that hostility until you reached the real man."

"That calls for a braver soul than mine," Glory answered softly. "And what makes you think Jesse is so wonderful, anyway? Some mothers would resent him, you know, for making their teenage daughter pregnant."

After dishing up two plates of spaghetti and meatballs and bringing them to the table, Delphine went back for salad, wine and garlic bread. Not until everything was ready and she'd taken her seat at the table did she respond. "Jesse had more privileges than you and Dylan did," she said in a thoughtful voice as she and Glory began to eat. "But he's had just as much unhappiness, if not more. First his parents died, then he lost the girl he loved, then Gresham and Sandy perished in that plane crash. I'll wager that on some level Jesse's afraid to let you know how much he still cares for you, thinking you'll either die or disappear again if he does."

Glory bit her lower lip for a moment to keep from crying. She'd done enough of that. "What makes you think Jesse still loves me?"

Delphine chuckled softly. "I *should* have realized it that first morning you were home. He watched you every single minute, except when you were looking at him, of course. And his rage tells me a lot, too. Fury isn't the opposite of love,

Glory—indifference is. And Jesse Bainbridge is *anything* but apathetic, where you're concerned."

Swallowing, Glory remembered the night she and Jesse had gone to dinner and ended up making love in his grandfather's car. His passion had been partly anger, but he'd taken the utmost care to please her. Still, when it was over, things hadn't been any different between them. "Face it, Mama. You were right in the first place—I should have stayed away from Jesse and Liza, even after I discovered the truth. Once your wedding was over, I could have gone on to San Francisco, and nobody would have been any the wiser where Liza's parenthood was concerned. I really blew it."

"I'm not so sure of that, darling. A little girl needs a mother, and there's no doubt that that child's been lonely, even though Jesse and Ilene have done their best by her."

Glory's throat thickened. "Big girls need their mothers, too, sometimes," she said, grateful that Delphine had come through when she needed her. Glory had wanted to be there for Liza, but she'd botched everything, and the damage seemed irreparable.

Delphine made a bed on Glory's sofa that night, and Glory slept better, knowing she wasn't alone. In the morning, though, her resolve was as firm as ever. She would make the necessary arrangements and leave Pearl River before she did anything else to hurt her child.

Since it would take time to orchestrate everything, Glory didn't give notice when she reported to work at the bank that morning. She just threw herself into her job and avoided every attempt anyone made at conversation. Everyone from Mr. Baker down to the lowliest file clerk, of course, was wondering exactly what had happened the day before, although most of them had probably gotten the general details by means of the grapevine.

After work she drove to the mall in Fawn Creek, where she bought Christmas presents for Liza, Jill, Ilene, and her mother and Harold. The bright decorations and happy music that had pleased her so much before, when she'd shopped with Liza, were a mockery now. She could hardly wait for the holiday to be over.

Later, at home, she wrapped each present with great care and placed them under the tree as she went. When the doorbell rang, her heart fluttered, but she knew better than to expect Jesse. He'd made his feelings perfectly clear the day Liza ran away.

When Glory pulled back the door, however, there he was.

"Delphine told me you're planning to leave," he said, and he might have been wearing his mirrored sunglasses, his eyes were so devoid of any emotion.

Glory nodded, knowing she should say something but unable to think of anything. And even if she'd managed that, it would have been hard to force words past the twisted knot in her throat.

"Could I come in?" She heard in Jesse's voice what she hadn't seen in his eyes; the effort he was making at self-control.

Still unable to speak, Glory stepped back, and he crossed the threshold warily, moving without his usual confidence and purpose to stand beside the Christmas tree.

Glory had just put a package underneath with Liza's name written on it in big gold letters, and she waited for him to say *his* daughter didn't need any presents from her. If he did, she knew she'd go at him like a wildcat, kicking and screaming and scratching.

But he only said, "Nice tree."

Reluctantly, Glory closed the door. "Thanks," she managed to croak.

He turned to face her. "Liza's doing okay," he said hoarsely.

Glory folded her arms, shielding her heart. "Good," she replied.

Jesse sighed. "I suppose it's for the best. Your leaving Pearl River, I mean."

Glory prayed she wouldn't cry. She had so little pride left as it was. "I suppose," she said.

He took a step toward her, and there was something tender in his eyes, behind the cautious expression she realized now had always been there, even when they were kids. "Glory," he murmured, and the name was a sentence in itself. It was a plea, a reprimand, a shout of fury, a kiss.

His hands rested on the sides of her waist, and Glory gave a despairing whimper, knowing that even now, with her world lying in pieces around her, her need for Jesse was as great as it had ever been.

He pulled her into his kiss and she went willingly, wrapping her arms around his neck. He cupped his powerful hands under her bottom and pressed her to him, while his tongue conquered hers.

"Jesse," she gasped, when he finally broke the kiss, but he didn't hear her. He lifted her T-shirt off over her head, and she let him—she let him because she knew this time was going to be the last, that it would have to sustain her for the rest of her life.

He pushed her bra down, without bothering to unsnap it, so that it rested around her waist in a gossamer pink circle, then lifted her high, so that her plump breasts were level with his face. Glory wrapped her legs around his lean hips and thrust her head back with a cry of relief and welcome when she felt his warm mouth close over a nipple.

Jesse was greedy at her breasts—it was as though he couldn't get enough of them. He went from one to the other, suckling, nibbling, nipping lightly with his teeth. But after a time, he carried Glory into her room and laid her on her unmade bed with her hips on the edge of the mattress.

She tossed her head from side to side and clutched at the sheets and blankets as he lowered her jeans and panties and then tossed them away, along with her shoes and stockings. Then he parted her legs and slid his hands under her bottom to raise her to his mouth.

When he captured her, she arched her back and clawed frantically at the bedclothes. The last bit of her pride was gone, shriveled to cinders in the heat of his passion. "Jesse—oh, yes—please—*Jesse*—"

He brought her swiftly to a scorching release, stroking her quivering bottom as she flailed under his tongue, stripping off his own clothes while she lay trembling in the aftermath of her satisfaction.

Jesse entered her in one powerful thrust, and she raised her hips to take him to her very depths. He buried his face in her neck as they moved together, now nibbling at the skin there, now raising his lips to her earlobe.

Glory threw herself against him with all the strength she had, desperate for the sweet union that would not be complete until she and Jesse collided in that final, explosive contact, their cries mingling in the velvety darkness of the night.

Jesse burst out with a ragged oath when passion finally overtook him, making him drive deep into Glory's body and remain there, trembling violently as she forced him to give up his seed. Beneath him, she sobbed his name, clasped her hands behind his head and dragged him into a kiss.

"We'll always have that to remember," he said a long time later, sitting up and reaching for his clothes, "if nothing else."

Glory pulled the covers up to her chin and stared at the darkened ceiling. It took all her remaining strength to say the words.

"Goodbye, Jesse."

10

Ilene Bainbridge's usually serene eyes flashed with annoyance and frustration. "*Grow up,* Jesse!" she snapped, making no effort to keep her voice down because the bookstore was empty of customers and Liza was still at school. "Here's a bulletin for you, Sheriff: you're not the first guy who's ever been hurt. And if you don't change some of your attitudes, you're going to end up a bitter, vindictive old man, just like Seth!"

Jesse stared at his cousin in amazement. He'd never seen her so angry. "Next you're going to tell me I should expect three ghosts to drop by tonight and point out the error of my ways," he said, trying to lighten the mood.

Ilene went back to unpacking a new shipment of books then, and her movements were still angry and abrupt. "Just go away, Jesse. I don't want to talk to you right now, because I'm going to end up saying a lot of things I'll regret."

He remained where he was, standing beside the counter with his arms folded. "What do you think

I should do?'' he asked quietly. Jesse wasn't one to let others dictate his opinions, but he had a lot of respect for Ilene. Ever since Gresham and Sandy's death, when custody of Liza had fallen to him, Ilene had been there to Ilprovide the female companionship the child needed.

She sighed heavily. ''That's not for me to say, Jesse. But if I were you, I'd examine my feelings very closely before I let Glory leave my life again. And I'd try to understand what it is to be eighteen and intimidated by a powerful man like Seth, and I'd be a little forgiving. After all, 'tis the season.''

Jesse's beeper went off just then and, frowning, he reached for the telephone behind the counter. Quickly he punched out his office number. ''Bainbridge,'' he said, when his secretary answered.

A car accident had been reported, five minutes north of town, the woman told him, and the State Patrol was shorthanded because of all the holiday travelers and the uncommonly heavy snow. They wondered if Jesse's department would take care of this one.

''Tell them I'm on my way,'' he said. ''Are there ambulances on the scene?''

''They're en route,'' the secretary answered, and Jesse thanked her and hung up.

''Merry Christmas,'' he said to Ilene in a distracted tone of voice, as he wrenched open the door of the bookshop and headed out into the cold.

Once he was inside the patrol car, he switched on the lights and siren and made a wide U-turn.

All during the drive, he braced himself for what he might find when he reached the scene of the accident. "Just don't let there be any kids," he muttered, in case some guardian angel was listening.

Liza came slowly toward Glory, who stood by the little Christmas tree they'd decorated together a few nights before, there in one corner of Ilene's cozy little bookshop. Glory was holding the presents she'd bought for her daughter in arms that trembled slightly.

"Hello, Glory," Liza said cautiously, as though speaking to a bird that might take flight at any instant. Ilene put the "closed" sign in place, locked the door, and retreated behind the counter to empty the cash register.

Glory held out the presents, and Liza accepted them shyly, with a murmured, "Thank you. I've got something for you, too, but it's upstairs."

Don't let me cry, Glory prayed desperately. *Please, just get me through this, and give Liza a happy life, and I won't ever ask You for anything else.* She waited, not trusting herself to speak, and the child hesitated, too, as though afraid that Glory would leave if she turned her back for a moment.

"You'll wait?" she asked. The slight quaver in the little girl's voice was almost Glory's undoing.

"I'll be right here," she said softly.

With that promise, Liza set the packages Glory had given her on the seat of the rocking chair and scampered upstairs.

Glory swallowed and turned her gaze toward Ilene, who was watching her. "I guess Liza's going to stay right here with you, even though she knows Jesse's her father," she said.

Ilene shook her head. "Jesse's hiring a nanny and a housekeeper," she said. "He wants Liza to live with him."

"Won't you miss her?" Glory asked, putting her hands in the pockets of her coat in an effort to keep them still.

Ilene smiled. "Of course I will. But I'll see her often."

Before Glory could say any more, Liza returned, proudly carrying a small box wrapped in red-and-white striped paper and tied with curling ribbons of both colors.

"Would you please open it right now?" the child asked.

Glory's heart caught at the carefully contained eagerness she heard in her daughter's voice. Unable to speak, for the moment at least, she began undoing the ribbon and paper. Inside a plain white box, nestled on a bed of cotton, lay a beautiful silver locket.

Sinking her teeth into her lower lip, Glory opened the locket and found a miniature photograph of Liza inside. Several awkward moments passed before she dropped to her knees and took the little girl into her arms. "Oh, Liza, thank you. It's the finest present I've ever had, and I'll wear it always. Whenever I touch it, I'll remember you."

Liza stepped back in Glory's embrace. "Remember me?" she echoed. "Are you going away?"

Glory felt the tears she'd sworn not to shed stinging her eyes. "Yes, baby."

"Why?" The word was plaintive, despairing, and it practically tore out of Glory's heart.

Glory took the time to put the locket around her neck and clasp it, needing those moments to get a new grip on her composure. Then she laid her hands on Liza's small shoulders. "Sweetheart, the things I'm going to say might be hard to understand, but I hope you'll try very hard, because it's so important.

"I love you, and I've thought of you every single day of the nine years since I turned you over to the adoption people. And there will never be a day in the future when I don't hold you in my heart and pray that you're happy and well.

"But I know now that it was a mistake for me to stay here in Pearl River, once I realized who you were. Sweetheart, all I've done is cause you trouble and pain, and I'd rather die than go on doing that. So I've got to go away."

"No!" Liza cried, twisting out of Glory's grasp only to fling frantic little arms around her neck.

"No! You're my mommy, and you can't go away and leave me—*please* don't—"

Glory held the child close. Walking out that door in a few minutes was going to be the hardest thing she'd ever done, more difficult even than leaving Liza the first time. But she and Jesse couldn't go on pulling their daughter back and forth between them. "Darling, I promise I'll write, and when you're older, if it's all right with your dad, you can come and visit me." She pulled back far enough to take Liza's quivering chin in her hand and look straight into her tear-filled eyes. "And I want a promise from you, too, Liza Bainbridge. I want your word that you won't ever, ever run away again."

"Glory, *please*—"

She swallowed and held her chin high. "Liza."

"I promise."

Glory kissed her daughter's forehead. "Good. I love you," she finished. And then she got slowly to her feet and went toward the door.

"Glory!" Liza wailed brokenly.

"God forgive me," Glory whispered, as she wrestled with the lock and then opened the door to go. The thought of Jesse came to her on the cold wind. "God forgive us both."

Without looking back, she hurried out into the dark, chilly night, half blinded by tears and grief.

Back home, she packed her suitcases, threw away all the food in the refrigerator, and took all the lights and ornaments off the Christmas tree.

Then, after taking a long, hot bath, she dressed and got into her car. Glory drove by Jill's place, but didn't stop, since she'd left an awkward farewell message on her friend's answering machine. And then she went past the diner.

Through the colorfully festooned windows, she saw Delphine and Harold presiding over a punch bowl full of eggnog, and the place was packed with friends. They were expecting Glory, but she couldn't bring herself to stop and go in. She'd telephone later, from somewhere down the road, and hope Delphine and Harold would understand why she was skipping out before their wedding.

There was just one more place she needed to go before leaving Pearl River forever. With a glance toward the little potted Christmas tree she'd bought at the supermarket earlier, Glory headed for the cemetery.

"Drunk driver," one of the ambulance attendants confided to Jesse when he arrived. The man paused after wrapping the patient in warm blankets and strapping him to the stretcher.

Jesse swore and scanned the scene, seeing a large car that looked relatively unmarked and a little one that appeared hopelessly battered. "How many people were hurt?"

"Just this guy," the attendant answered. "He's had a few too many, and his head's banged up pretty good, but my guess is he'll be out of the hospital in time to have turkey dinner with his family tomorrow."

"If he was driving with more than the legal limit of alcohol in his blood," Jesse said quietly, "he's going to spend Christmas in the county jail. Have you got a reading?"

The attendant gave Jesse a number that made him swear again and handed him the man's driver's license. After checking the identification, he bent over and looked down into the party boy's face. "Hey, buddy," he began jovially, "I want to wish you a Merry Christmas on behalf of the Pearl River County sheriff's department. I'm here to offer you our hospitality, since as soon as they're done with you over at the emergency room, we'll be coming by to pick you up. You have the right to remain silent, Mr. Callahan. Anything you say can and will be used against you in a court of law..."

"You don't understand, Sheriff," Mr. Callahan whined, when Jesse had finished reading him his rights. "I only had a couple of eggnogs. Damn it, it's Christmas!"

"Ho, ho, ho," Jesse replied. And then he turned his attention to the shaken family huddled in the small, dented car on the side of the road.

He walked over, smiled and bent to look through the window as the driver rolled down the glass and said, "Hello, officer."

Jesse saw two kids with freckles and pigtails sitting in the back seat, clutching their dolls and looking scared, and silently thanked the benevolent fates for sparing them. "Merry Christmas," he said. "Is everybody sure they're okay?"

The driver, a man about Jesse's age, sighed. "We're fine," he said. "Just a little shaken up, that's all."

"How about the car? Does it run?"

The Christmas traveler shook his head. "The ambulance people radioed for a wrecker," he said. "But there probably won't be room in the cab for all four of us, and it's getting pretty cold in here."

Jesse nodded and thrust his hands into the pockets of his jacket. "I'll drive you into town," he said. "But before we go, I need you to tell me exactly what happened here. Is somebody expecting you in Pearl River?"

The woman leaned forward and smiled wanly, and Jesse watched her for signs of shock. "My grandmother, Alice Northrup. She's probably been watching the road ever since noon."

Jesse didn't remember the woman in the car, but he knew right where to find her grandmother. Miss Alice was a little old blue-haired lady who was always hearing prowlers in the her backyard. He grinned and opened the door so the little girls in back could get out. "I'll radio the office and have them get in touch with her," he said.

The children looked up at him with serious faces. "Are we arrested?" one of them asked.

The young parents laughed affectionately, but Jesse squatted down to look straight into the child's eyes. "No, ma'am," he said. "If I were to do a thing like that, Santa Claus would be real put out. And he's one man I don't like to cross."

"We've got presents in the trunk," said the other little girl.

Jesse settled the woman and the two kids and the presents in the patrol car, with the heater going full blast, then radioed the office. Deputy Johnson promised to let Mrs. Northrup know that her loved ones were safe and would be arriving soon.

While the three females sang Christmas carols, Jesse and the husband went over the accident scene. Soon, Jesse's report was complete, and he drove the family to Grandma's house.

He felt a little envious, watching the old woman run out to greet them. That was what Christmas was all about, he thought to himself, and wondered why he couldn't get things right in his own life.

Stopping by the office, he left the report to be typed by Deputy Johnson, who'd drawn duty that night, took a package from the top drawer of his desk, and went back to his car.

The lights of a huge tree were visible through the big front window of the nursing home when Jesse arrived, and he heard the voices of carolers from one of the churches as he came up the walk. The residents, male and female alike, were gathered around the main room, singing, their faces splashed with color.

Jesse smiled and greeted a few of the patients as he worked his way through the room toward the hallway. He'd known without looking that his grandfather wouldn't be among the merrymakers; Seth had never cared much about Christmas.

Reaching the door of the judge's room, Jesse paused and knocked.

"Come in," grumbled a familiar voice.

Jesse went in grinning. "Well," he said, going to stand beside his grandfather's bed, "if it isn't Scrooge himself. Merry Christmas, Gramps."

"Humph!" said Gramps, but he reached out for the present Jesse had brought. "Probably slippers. Or another box of chocolates."

"Wrong," Jesse replied easily, dropping into a chair. He wanted to be home with Liza and Ilene—how he wished Glory would be there, too—but he loved this old coot, for all his cantankerous ways.

The judge ripped open the paper to reveal a kit for building a ship in a bottle. Despite his effort to appear singularly unimpressed, he opened the instructions with fumbling, awkward fingers and peered at them. "Get me my glasses!" he snapped.

Jesse chuckled and took the familiar leather case out of the drawer beside Seth's bed, handing him the bifocals. "I figure it'll take you till next Christmas to put the thing together," he teased. "Then you can just wrap it up and give it back to me."

Seth laughed, in spite of himself. "The hell I will," he said. "Don't you have anything better to do on Christmas Eve besides pick on an old man?"

Sadness touched Jesse's spirit as he thought of Glory again. "I can hang around for a while," he told his grandfather quietly.

"That woman still in town?"

Jesse felt his hackles rise, but he reminded himself that it was Christmas, that Liza and Ilene were waiting for him at the mansion, and that Alice Northrup's family had made it home, safe and sound, to hang up their stockings. Maybe that was all he could ask of the holiday. "You mean Glory?" he asked.

Seth nodded.

"She's leaving soon," Jesse said, and the words left him feeling raw and hollow inside.

"I paid her off, you know."

"Yes, Gramps," Jesse sighed. "I know."

"Told her I'd send that brother of hers straight to jail if she didn't leave you alone," the judge reflected proudly.

Jesse sat bolt upright in his chair, feeling as though somebody had just goosed him with a cattle prod. *"What?"* he rasped. "You involved Dylan in this?"

The judge chuckled, obviously reveling in his own cleverness. "He was a troublemaker. It would have been easy to have him sent up."

Standing now, Jesse gripped the lapels of the old man's bathrobe. He didn't want to scare him, just get his undivided attention. *"You told Glory if she didn't leave, you were going to frame Dylan?"*

Seth nodded, his beetle eyebrows rising a notch. He looked somewhat less amused. "I wanted to protect you, Jesse. And she wasn't going to take the money. I had to do something—"

"Fool," Jesse rasped, turning away, and he wasn't talking to the judge. He was talking to himself. "You damn fool!"

"Now, Jesse, I—"

It was too late for the old man; he'd probably go to his grave believing he'd done the right thing. But Jesse still had time to undo some of his mistakes, and he didn't want to waste a minute.

"Merry Christmas," he said, excited as a kid, giving Seth a quick, affectionate slap on the back. "I'll come out tomorrow and make sure you eat all your turkey and stuffing. But right now, I've got to go!"

"Hey, wait a—"

Jesse was gone before the sentence was completed, striding down the hall, joining a chorus of "God Rest Ye Merry Gentlemen" as he hurried through the main room and out into that cold, snowy Christmas Eve.

He went to Glory's apartment first, breaking the speed limit all the way, but when he pulled up out front, her windows were dark. She was probably with Delphine, over at the diner.

Making a wide turn, Jesse bumped the tires over the sidewalk on the other side of the street and sped toward Delphine's.

There were people jammed inside the diner—mostly folks who didn't have anywhere to go—and carols were being sung at ear-splitting volume. Jesse waded through the crowd until he found Delphine, gripped her gently by one elbow, and hustled her into the kitchen.

"Where's Glory?" he demanded.

Delphine glanced at her watch and frowned. "I don't know. She should have been here by now. I'd better call."

Jesse's throat felt tight for a moment, then he managed to grind out, "I was just at her place. It was dark as a mole's fruit cellar."

Glory's mother gave him an accusing look. "She's been depressed lately," she said pointedly. Then she marched over to the wall phone and punched out her daughter's number. A long time passed before she hung up, her teeth sunk into her lower lip, her brows drawn together.

Before Jesse could say anything else, Jill appeared in the doorway. "I come bearing sad tidings," she said dismally. "It's bad news, bears."

"What?" Jesse snapped.

Jill glared at him. "Don't you get smart with me, Jesse Bainbridge. As far as I'm concerned, this whole thing is your fault!"

"Jill, please," Delphine pleaded, her voice small, and Jill put an arm around her.

"When I came home from doing some last-minute shopping just a few minutes ago, there was a message from Glory on my answering machine. She said she hoped everybody would understand, but she had to leave Pearl River while she still had some of her soul left." Jill paused to narrow her eyes at Jesse, holding Delphine tightly against her side. "She left for San Francisco tonight."

Delphine looked as if she was going to cry, and Jesse hadn't seen her do that since that night ten years before, when he'd come to her half drunk and begged her to tell him where Glory was. "Without saying goodbye to Harold and me?" she whispered disbelievingly.

"I'm sure she means to call you later tonight," Jill said comfortingly.

"I guess Glory isn't very good at saying goodbye to anybody," Jesse muttered, and then he left the diner by the back way, unable to face any more holiday cheer.

As he slipped behind the wheel of the patrol car, soft, fat flakes of snow began to fall.

"You're not getting away with it this time, Glory," he whispered, reaching for his radio mike. He contacted the office, and got the long-suffering Deputy Johnson. "Call my place, will you, and ask Ilene if Glory's been by."

"Roger," replied the deputy.

A few minutes later, as Jesse was cruising the main street of town, the answer came. Glory had stopped by the bookstore briefly, just about closing time. She'd said goodbye to Liza and left.

Swearing, Jesse pulled over to the side of the road and went into a phone booth. One quarter and three long rings later, Ilene answered his telephone at home.

"Bainbridge residence. This is Ilene."

"How is Liza?" Jesse blurted, rubbing his eyes with the thumb and forefinger of one hand.

Ilene sighed. "She's doing okay for somebody who's lost two mothers and one father."

"What the hell did Glory say to her?"

"She said she loved her," Ilene answered somewhat acidly. "Terrible woman."

"Damn it, Ilene, I don't need this right now. I just found out that Gramps forced her into leaving town ten years ago by threatening to throw her brother in jail. I've got to find her."

"Are you thinking what I hope you're thinking?"

"If—*when* I find Glory, I'm going to admit I'm an idiot and beg her forgiveness. And then I'll propose, and if she says yes, we'll go drag Judge Jordal away from home and hearth to issue us a special license and perform the marriage ceremony."

"That would be one jim-dandy Christmas miracle if you could pull it off," Ilene said eagerly. "Good luck, Jesse."

"Thanks," Jesse said, and even though he was grinning like a fool, his voice came out sounding hoarse.

The cemetery was well-lighted, and Glory wasn't surprised to see other people visiting lost loved ones on Christmas Eve. It was the most difficult time of year for the bereaved.

She dusted the snow off Dylan's headstone and then put the little potted tree in front of it. "Merry Christmas," she said, putting one hand to her throat and sniffling once. She squatted down beside the grave and rested one hand against the cold marble stone.

"I know, I know," she said. "I've got to quit hanging around here this way. But you must remember how I was always tagging after you." Glory took a tissue from her coat pocket, dried her eyes and dabbed at her nose. She sighed, and a smile crept across her face. "Remember that Christmas when we hid flashlights under our mattresses and practically synchronized our watches so we could peek at the presents after Mama put them out? You got a baseball glove, and I got one of those dolls that talked when you pulled the string.''

Suddenly Glory began to cry. Hard. She put her hands over her eyes and sobbed.

''There now, miss,'' said a kindly voice, and strong fingers closed around Glory's shoulders and lifted her to her feet. ''I like to think them that went before are having Christmas tonight, too, somewhere.''

Stunned, Glory lowered her hands to stare into a gentle, weathered old face. ''Who are you?''

''Name's Clyde Ballard,'' the elderly gentleman said, touching the brim of his snow-dusted fedora. ''My wife Sylvia is buried out here, and I like to come by of a Christmas Eve and leave her a poinsettia plant. She always loved those pretty red blossoms, and she could make 'em bloom year after year, too. Used to fill our living room with the things.''

Glory dried her eyes with the back of one mitten, since she'd already exhausted her tissue supply, and squinted at the man. He didn't look familiar. ''You must miss her very much,'' she said, a little ashamed of her outburst a few minutes before.

''Oh, I certainly do,'' agreed Mr. Ballard, bending to read the words and dates on Dylan's stone. ''And you miss this young fellow, too. It's a pity he died so early.''

Glory nodded. She was beginning to feel better. "He was killed in an explosion a couple of months after he joined the air force."

"That's real sad," said Mr. Ballard sincerely. "But I know he wouldn't want you here in the graveyard, crying your pretty eyes out, on Christmas Eve!"

Glory chuckled. "You're right about that."

"Of course I am," the old man responded. "I'm on my way over to Delphine's Diner for some pecan pie and eggnog. You ought to come along— there's always room for one more when *she* throws a party."

Nodding, Glory smiled. "I know," she answered.

Mr. Ballard started to say something else, but just as he opened his mouth, Glory saw a patrol car pull up down by the gates, lights flashing. Her heart surged into her throat.

"Jesse," she whispered.

Mr. Ballard gave a pleased cackle. "You wanted for some crime, young lady?" he teased.

"I'm an incorrigible jaywalker," Glory confided, and Mr. Ballard laughed.

"I'd better run along before the pie's all gone. You sure you don't want to come along?"

Impulsively Glory kissed his cheek. "Maybe I'll be by later," she said. Her heartbeat was loud and fast now, pounding in her ears. "Merry Christmas, Mr. Ballard."

"Merry Christmas to you, little lady," he responded. He passed Jesse on his way down the hill and touched the brim of his hat in that same courtly manner as before.

Jesse didn't even seem to see Mr. Ballard; he was looking up at Glory. Reaching her, he took her shoulders in his hands.

"I thought you left for the money," he said gruffly. "But tonight Gramps told me he threatened to have Dylan framed for some crime if you stayed."

"Or if I said so much as a word to you," Glory clarified, swallowing. "What are you doing here, Jesse?"

He grasped her hand and led her to a nearby bench. After dusting off some of the snow so she could sit, Jesse pressed her onto the bench and dropped to one knee in front of her. Snow and mud were probably seeping through his pant leg, but he didn't seem to care. "Glory, I was wrong. I was stubborn and prideful, and you were right when you said I was only thinking of myself. Will you forgive me? Please?"

Glory blinked, uncertain that any of this was really happening. Maybe it was all an illusion. "Well—okay."

Jesse gave a jubilant burst of laughter, rising to his feet and hauling Glory with him. He put his arms around her and kissed her thoroughly. "I love you," he said when it was over.

She stared up at him. This was real, all right. No fantasy kiss had ever felt like that. "Well, I love you, too, but—"

He laid a finger to her lips. "But nothing. Will you marry me, Glory? Now—tonight?"

She kissed the tip of his finger and then reluctantly shook her head. "No, Jesse. We have too many things to work out. But I'll marry you in the summer if you still want me."

Jesse held her close, and it felt impossibly good. His lips moved against her temple. "But you won't leave again—you'll stay right here in Pearl River?"

Glory cupped her hands on either side of his face, feeling a new beard scratch against her palms. "I'll stay, Jesse. I promise," she said, and then she stood on tiptoe to kiss him.

11

The lights of the Bainbridge mansion glowed golden through the snowy night, and as the patrol car reached the top of the driveway, the door burst open and a small silhouette appeared in the opening.

"Today Ilene told me to grow up," Jesse confessed hoarsely, as he brought the car to a stop in front of the garage, "and I think I finally have. No matter what happens between us over the next six months, Glory, Liza is your child as much as mine, and I won't ever try to keep you away from her again."

Glory squeezed his hand and pushed open the car door. "Liza!" she called in a happy sob.

The little girl scrambled toward her, her voice shrill with surprise and delight. "Glory, *you came back*!"

Glory enfolded her daughter in her arms and held her close, right there in Jesse's snowy yard. "I'll stay if you want me to," she managed to whisper.

"Oh, baby, I'm so sorry for the trouble I've caused—I never meant to hurt you..."

Liza pulled back in Glory's embrace and looked up at her, and for a moment it was as though their roles were reversed, and Glory was the child. "I understand, Mom. Aunt Ilene explained about all the things that happened to make you and Uncle Jesse—Dad—unhappy."

The word "Mom" had brought a sheen of tears to Glory's eyes. "Here you are, outside without a coat," she scolded good-naturedly. "Let's get inside before you catch pneumonia."

The interior of the mansion was decorated with cheerful good taste. The scent of a live tree filled the air, and instrumental Christmas music provided a cozy background.

Ilene came forward to kiss Glory soundly on the forehead, Jesse on the cheek. "It's about time," she said, and then, claiming she had to baste tomorrow's turkey, she disappeared into the kitchen.

Jesse put one hand on Glory's back and one on Liza's and ushered his family into the huge living room, where an enormous tree towered in one corner and a fire snapped on the hearth. He took Glory's coat and laid it aside before removing his own and squatting down to look into Liza's eyes.

She was seated in one of the leather wing chairs, her face shining brightly enough to rival the star of Bethlehem. "You're going to marry Mom," she said with the confidence of a seasoned game show contestant.

Jesse glanced back at Glory over one shoulder and grinned before facing his daughter again. "Yeah, I'm going to marry her. But how did you know? Things have been pretty bad lately."

"I wished it, that's why. And I asked my other mommy and daddy to talk to God about it special. After all, they're angels, and they're right there in heaven with Him."

Glory's throat was tight again. She perched on the arm of Liza's chair and laid a hand on her shoulder. The beautiful man and child before her blurred for a moment.

Jesse reached out and tugged affectionately at one of Liza's braids. "I'm sorry I was so bull-headed, sweetheart," he said, his voice low and a little husky. "Will you forgive me?"

She threw her small arms around his neck. "Sure I will, Dad!" she crowed. "I'm not some imma-ture kid, you know!"

Jesse laughed and held her tightly, but the look in his eyes was strictly for Glory, and so was the saucy wink. "I think you'd better call Delphine," he said after a few moments. "Jill reported you of-ficially missing from the fold, and it didn't exactly make your mother's Christmas."

Glory nodded and scanned the room for a tele-phone. There was one sitting on a desk over by one of the towering windows. She dialed the number at the diner and fiddled with the silver locket Liza had given her earlier, while she waited.

Delphine answered almost immediately, and she sounded breathless. "Hello?"

"Mama, it's me, Glory."

"Mr. Ballard said he saw you at the cemetery!" Delphine cried. "Sweetheart, are you all right?"

Glory lifted her eyes and saw Jesse sitting in the wing chair, with Liza balanced happily on his knee. "Oh, I'm more than all right, Mama. Jesse and I have agreed to try to work things out, and I'm staying here in Pearl River. With any luck, I'll be a bride this summer."

It was plain that Delphine was crying, and that her tears were happy ones. "Oh, darling, that's wonderful."

"And Jesse has promised not to try to keep me away from Liza even if we don't end up as a family."

"You will," Delphine said with certainty. "I swear, this Christmas is just like in the movies. I wouldn't be at all surprised if there was an angel involved somewhere."

Glory watched her daughter's glowing, animated face. "There's an angel involved, all right. Merry Christmas, Mama. I'll see you sometime tomorrow."

Delphine made a sound she called "kiss-kiss," bid her daughter a magical night, and hung up.

Liza was about to hang up her stocking, when Glory returned from making a call. It was an enormous thing, almost as tall as its owner. Jesse lifted his daughter by the waist so she could reach one of the special hooks set into the underside of the mantel.

The knowledge of those hooks eased a tightness in Glory's heart. Knowing Seth Bainbridge had once been a little boy, eagerly hanging a stocking above this same fireplace, washed away the last of the bitterness she'd held toward the old man. Even better was the relative certainty that other Bainbridge children would celebrate their Christmases here, too. Her children and Jesse's.

"I've got to get back to work," Jesse said with a sigh when he'd set Liza on her feet again.

Liza nodded, evidently used to his erratic schedule. Then her eyes shifted to Glory. "You'll stay, won't you? You'll be here in the morning, when I wake up?"

Under any other circumstances, Glory would have gently refused. She didn't have any compunctions at all about sleeping with Jesse—as far as she was concerned, he was already her mate—but she hadn't planned on sharing his bed with Liza in the same house until after the wedding. Still, Liza had been through a great deal in her young life, and she deserved to have her mother nearby on this special night.

"I'll stay," Glory said with a shy glance at Jesse.

His dark eyes smoldered with teasing passion as he gazed at her, making a blush rise from her breasts to her face. After kissing Liza good-night and sending her off to find a favorite storybook, Jesse took Glory's hand and pulled her close to him. "I'm going to make very thorough love to you tonight," he vowed quietly.

Glory trembled against him, feeling the promises his body was making to hers. "Jesse—"

"I know," he interrupted, his lips almost upon hers. "It's only for tonight, and you're not moving in until after the wedding. Which is not to say I won't have you at *your place* whenever I get the chance." He kissed her, his tongue seeking entrance to her mouth with gentle insistence and then breaking down the barriers to conquer her utterly and give her a foretaste of what awaited her.

When he finally released her, Glory was clinging to the front of his shirt with both hands just so she wouldn't slide to the floor. "D-do you still sleep in the same room?"

Jesse grinned. "No, ma'am. That room is Liza's now. I'm in the big master suite at the other end of the hall."

Glory blushed and swallowed. Where this man was concerned, she had no pride, at all. But then, she'd always known that. "I'll be there waiting when you get home, Jesse," she promised.

He took a teasing nibble at her lower lip before responding, "Don't expect one ride over the moon and the proverbial long winter's nap," he warned, his voice throaty and low. "We've got a lot of time to make up, and I intend to show you what you've missed."

She let her forehead rest against his shoulder for a moment, then looked up at him with a soft smile. "You enjoy the idea that I'll be thinking about all the things we're going to do, and wanting them, don't you?"

"Yes," he answered without hesitation, and then he kissed her again, swatted her once on the bottom and went out.

Moments later, Liza returned, her storybook gripped in both hands. "Will you read this to me, please?" she asked hopefully. "It's *A Visit From St. Nicholas.*"

Sitting down in Jesse's chair and pulling the child onto her lap, Glory uttered a silent prayer of thanks and began to read. Ilene crept in, with hot buttered rums for both herself and Glory, and listened to the old favorite with a smile on her face.

When she'd completed the poem, Glory just sat, reveling in the fact that she was holding the daughter she'd once thought she'd never see again. It was pure bliss knowing they wouldn't have to be separated anymore. And then there was the sweet certainty that later, when the presents had been set out and Christmas Day was about to dawn, Jesse would take her to his bed and make love to her.

Presently, Liza laid her head against Glory's shoulder and yawned hugely.

"I think somebody needs to say good-night," Ilene observed gently.

Liza looked up at Glory's face. "But you won't go away, will you, Mom?"

Glory touched the tip of Liza's nose with an index finger. "I won't go away," she promised. "Not only that, but I'll tuck you in and hear your prayers, too."

A few minutes later, mother and daughter climbed the stairs, with their intricately carved banister. Jesse's old room had been so thoroughly changed that Glory wouldn't have recognized it. Pink-and-gold striped paper covered the walls, and there was a four-poster, billowing with lace and ruffles, where Jesse's waterbed had been. Teddy bears and dolls lined the window seat, instead of model airplanes and copies of *Popular Mechanix*.

After brushing her teeth and putting on a flannel nightgown in the small adjoining bathroom, Liza knelt down beside the bed, and Glory took a place beside her.

"Thank you, God, for letting me have a mom and dad again. And thank you that it's Christmas. You've been real good to me, so if Santa Claus—" Liza paused here to looking meaningfully at Glory, letting her know she was speaking in the figurative sense "—if Santa Claus doesn't bring me a Nintendo game or a Prom Date Barbie, I'll be perfectly happy. Good night, God, and Merry Christmas."

Glory rested her forehead against her folded hands for a few moments to hide the tears in her eyes. Although they sprang from joy, not sorrow, she was afraid Liza would misunderstand them and be worried. "Thank you, God," she echoed in a broken voice.

After that, Liza climbed into bed, and Glory tucked the covers in around her and gave her a sound good-night kiss.

"I'm so glad you came back," the child whispered.

"Me, too," Glory answered, her voice shaking. "I love you, sweetheart."

"I love—you," Liza replied, stopping once to yawn.

Downstairs, Glory found that Ilene had reheated her buttered rum, and she raised it gratefully to her lips. "This has been quite some day," she told her friend.

Ilene smiled. "Yes, it has." She paused to sip from her cup and gaze at the glowing embers in the fire. "Jesse was planning to roust Judge Jordal from his bed and force him to marry the two of you this very night."

Glory laughed as an image of Jesse strong-arming an old man in a flowing nightshirt and matching cap filled her mind. "We've agreed to wait six months before we get married. Not that I have any doubts. I want to show Jesse that I'm in for the duration this time."

Ilene reached out to pat her hand. "You're a wise woman, Glory Parsons. By the time June rolls around, our stubborn Jesse should be in a very flexible frame of mind."

The two women sat and talked for about an hour, and then Ilene excused herself. "Liza will be up early, tearing into the presents," she said. "Therefore, I'm off to get whatever sleep I can."

Glory nodded and, when Ilene had been gone for a few minutes, she went to the fireplace and threw in another chunk of wood.

A little after midnight, Jesse returned, smiling when he saw Glory sitting there, enjoying the quiet, the fire and the lights on the tree.

He approached and pulled her out of the chair just long enough to sit in it himself. Then he placed her carefully on his lap. "I stopped a fat guy for speeding tonight on my way home," he told her, looking solemn as he traced her jawline with a chilly finger. "He was driving a sleigh, if you can believe it, pulled by eight tiny reindeer."

Glory laughed, thinking if she loved this man any more, she'd burst like an overfilled balloon. "I *don't* believe it, Sheriff. I think you must have been hallucinating."

He shifted and pulled a small velvet box out of the pocket of his coat. "If I was hallucinating," he reasoned, "how come he gave me this?"

Glory stared at the object. "Is that . . . ?"

Jesse attempted to look very exasperated. "Of course it isn't the same ring I bought for Adara. Don't you think I have any class, at all? I persuaded Harvey Milligan to open the jewelry store." He set the box in her palm.

Her fingers trembled slightly as she lifted the lid. Immediately a cluster of diamonds caught the lights of the Christmas tree and the flicker of the fire and held them fast. "Oh, Jesse, it's beautiful."

He took the ring out of its little slot and slid it onto her finger. Only then did he ask, "Will you marry me, Glory?"

She kissed him, treating him to previews of coming attractions. "Yes," she finally answered. "Next June, just like we planned."

Jesse sighed philosophically. "Next June," he agreed. Then he gave Glory a swat and set her on her feet. "Let's get busy, wife-of-Christmas-future. We've got a stocking to fill, and toys to set out. Then I'm going to take you upstairs and do right by you."

He peeled off his jacket and tossed it aside, then removed his gun and holster and locked them carefully away.

Glory had never had so much fun as she did filling Liza's stocking with an orange and a candy cane and a variety of other goodies. She helped Jesse set out the video-game center Liza had wanted, along with the Barbie doll she'd asked for, a set of delicate little china dishes and a huge stuffed horse.

Jesse and Glory stood holding hands for a while, admiring their handiwork, then Jesse checked the screen on the fireplace and turned out the Christmas-tree lights. Glory was caught by surprise when he swept her into his arms, Rhett Butler-style, and carried her up the stairs and along the hallway.

The master suite was enormous, with its own wood-burning fireplace and room enough for a couch and two chairs, not to mention the bed. There was a table, too, beside bay windows, and Glory dreamed of sitting there, watching the moonlight play on the snow.

"Do you always work nights?" Glory asked.

Jesse set her down and immediately started unbuttoning his uniform shirt. "My hours are crazy," he sighed. "Sometimes it's nights, sometimes it's days, sometimes it's twenty-four or forty-eight hours straight." He bent his head and nipped at one of Glory's nipples, causing it to push against the fabric of her bra. "I guess you're just going to have to figure I'm going to be making love to you at some very weird times. I can promise you one thing, Glory—it'll happen often. Want to share my shower?"

Glory nodded, and her eyes drifted closed as Jesse began unbuttoning her shirt. He stripped her slowly, pausing to kiss and nibble on everything he bared, and Glory was trembling by the time he took her hand and led her into the bathroom.

After making sure both spigots in the double shower were spraying warm water, Jesse stepped into the stall and pulled Glory after him.

She knew if she didn't take the lead right away, Jesse would, so she reached for the soap and a large sponge and began to wash him gently. He gave a low groan and braced himself against the wall of the shower with both hands when she reached his manhood and knelt to rinse him under the spray.

He cried out like some magnificent, wounded beast when she began treating him to some very deliberate attentions. "So long," he moaned after several moments of hard breathing. "Oh, God, Glory, it's been so long..."

"Ssh," she soothed, and then she made a circle with her tongue and Jesse's buttocks tensed under her hands.

He pleaded raggedly, and she gave him what he asked for, along with a series of little bites and kisses calculated to drive him crazy. Finally, in a fever, he hauled Glory to her feet and devoured her mouth in a kiss that left no doubt who was in charge.

She was dazed when he'd finished, and nothing could have made her protest when he turned her and set her hands on the steel safety bar affixed to the inside of the shower. He set her legs apart, and she drew in a deep breath because she knew actual intercourse with Jesse was going to be better than anything her fantasies could offer up.

His hands caressed her naked breasts for a few moments, then went to her hips, holding her firmly, setting her in position. "Do you want me, Glory?" he asked, his lips moving against her neck, the warm water streaming over both of them.

"Oh, yes," she answered. "Yes, Jesse." And she felt him at the center of her femininity, seeking entrance.

He gave her an inch of himself, just enough to tease. She was expanding to take him in, and the sensation was urgent and sweet. He continued to taste her neck. "I could make you wait," he reflected sleepily. "I could make you wait for a long time."

"No, Jesse—I want you—I need you *now*—" Because she was not without power herself, Glory gave a little twist of her hips and wrung a long groan from Jesse's throat.

He muttered words of surrender, and love, and then he drove deep into her, and she welcomed him with a gasp of joy.

At first their movements were slow and measured, but as the friction of that most intimate contact increased moment by moment, passion drove them before it, like a giant, swelling tide threatening to swallow them up.

When they were breathless from the chase, Jesse suddenly stiffened and uttered a warrior's low cry, his hands tightening over Glory's breasts. Glory felt his warmth spilling deep inside her and welcomed him, and in the next instant she went soaring over the precipice herself. Hoisted high on his shaft, his fingers working her nipples, Glory quivered repeatedly and then collapsed against the shower wall, exhausted.

But just as he'd promised, Jesse was far from through with her. He vowed to spend fifty years making up for the ten they'd sacrificed to pride and youth, and Glory looked forward to every minute.

After they'd gently washed and dried each other, Jesse took his bride-to-be to his bed and laid her there, watching the firelight play over her skin with solemn, hungry eyes. "You're so beautiful," he rasped, "and I need you so much."

Glory put her hands behind his head and pressed him to her breast, where he drank hungrily, while his fingers trailed over her thighs. Presently, Jesse caught Glory's hands together and held them high above her head, and she whimpered at being made more vulnerable to him.

It was only the beginning of vulnerabilities, and of pleasure. Over the course of that night, Glory surrendered again and again as Jesse put her through her paces, changing their positions and his demands regularly. Sometimes it was Jesse who submitted, but more often it was Glory.

And during those brief moments when her thoughts were at all coherent, she wondered how she had survived ten years without Jesse tuning her body and then causing it to play symphonies.

They slept for an hour, but then Jesse awakened Glory in a most delicious way and had her thoroughly, all over again. She was allowed to shower in peace only when Liza was up and around.

Her suitcase was lying on the bed when she came out wrapped in a towel.

"I stopped by your car and picked this up on the way home last night," Jesse said, watching her with those brazen brown eyes of his. "Can you imagine the speculation that must be going on? I can hear it now: 'I tell you, Mavis, she parked her car at the graveyard and disappeared without a trace.'"

Glory laughed and took out clean underwear, a pair of jeans and a roomy aqua-blue cable-knit sweater. "Give the gossips their due, Jesse," she said, beginning to dress. "They're saying I've been in your bed all night, and they're right."

He stopped her as she would have hooked her bra and gave each nipple a warm suckling before snapping the front catch himself and pulling the straps up onto her shoulders. "I love you, Glory."

Her cheeks heated as she looked up at him because, after all of it, she found herself wanting him to lay her back on the bed and take her again. She didn't know how she was going to wait six months to share this room with him on a regular basis, but she was determined to do it, because she wanted their marriage to be long and unshakably solid. "Oh, Jesse, I'm so wanton."

Jesse laughed. "Patience, Glory. There's always tonight at your place."

She smiled and put her arms around his neck to kiss him, teasing his lips with her tongue. "Since it's my bed, Sheriff," she said, "I'm going to be calling all the shots."

Reluctantly Jesse backed away, but not before Glory lightly touched the front of his jeans and found him reaching for her.

They went downstairs separately, Glory first, and Jesse about five minutes later.

It snowed on New Year's Eve, but that didn't stop Harold and Delphine's guests from attending the wedding. The church was still decorated with poinsettia plants from Christmas, and candlelight flickered romantically.

Glory stood at the front of the church, wearing her royal-blue bridesmaid's dress. Happy tears dropped into her bouquet of roses and carnations, and soon the vows had been exchanged and the bride and groom were hurrying down the aisle to strains of joyful music. As Glory turned to follow, she made eye contact with the man who would be her groom when summer came, and six months seemed to be a very long time.

On the other hand, when you compared it to forever, half a year was nothing. Glory and Jesse had arranged for special counseling with the pastor, for themselves and for Liza, and they were already working hard at learning to be a family.

She'd messed up badly once, and Glory didn't intend to make the same mistake again. She knew now that love doesn't just happen, it has to be nurtured and cared for.

Jesse was waiting at the foot of the aisle, his arm out for Glory, and she went into its curve willingly. "I'll drive you over to the reception," he whispered into her ear, managing to trace it once with the tip of his tongue, "but I can't promise to take the most direct route."

Glory was grateful that everyone was looking at Delphine, who made a lovely bride in her pale rose dress and big picture hat, because she herself was blushing. "Jesse Bainbridge," she scolded. But she let him put her into his grandfather's fancy car, and she didn't say a single word when he turned off down a sideroad and headed for the rest area overlooking the river.

Her protests were cut off with a kiss that made her go damp all over, and when Jesse made the seat go back, she just went with it, already too weak to sit up without support.

"Jesse, they'll miss us—my mother's wedding—"

"We'll be back in plenty of time for the pictures and the cake," Jesse said, raising her billowy skirt to find her with his hand and caress her.

Instinctively, Glory raised her knees up, then let them fall wide apart. Her hands gripped the tufted seats as Jesse ducked under her skirt and petticoats to tease her through the thin, tautly drawn panty hose. When he peeled them down, there were no protests from Glory, because he'd already created a need that made it hard for her to lie still.

He parted her, and she heard his muffled chuckle under all those ruffles. She would have sworn he said, "Glory, Glory, Hallelujah!"

*   *   *   *   *

Mr. and Mrs. Harold Seemer
request the honor of your presence
at the marriage of their daughter,
Glory Ann Parsons,
to Mr. Jesse Alexander Bainbridge
on Saturday
June twenty-second
at 2:00 p.m.
First Lutheran Church
Pearl River, Oregon

New York Times bestselling author

LINDA LAEL MILLER

Two separate worlds, denied by destiny.

THERE AND NOW

Elizabeth McCartney returns to her centuries-old family home in search of refuge—never dreaming escape would lie over a threshold. She is taken back one hundred years into the past and into the bedroom of the very handsome Dr. Jonathan Fortner, who demands an explanation from his T-shirt-clad "guest."

But Elizabeth has no *reasonable* explanation to offer.

Available in July 1997 at your favorite retail outlet.

Take 3 of "The Best of the Best™" Novels FREE

Plus get a FREE surprise gift!

Jake wasn't sure why he'd agreed to take the place
of his twin brother, nor why he'd agreed to commit
Nathan's crime. Maybe it was misplaced loyalty.

by *New York Times* bestselling author

After surviving a plane crash, Jake wakes up in a hospital
room and can't remember anything—or anyone...
including one very beautiful woman who comes to see
him. His wife. Caitlin. Who watches him so guardedly.

Her husband seems like a stranger to Caitlin—he's full of
warmth and passion. Just like the man she thought she'd
married. Until his memory returns. And with it, a danger
that threatens them all.

Available in February 1997 at your favorite retail outlet.

MIRA The brightest star in women's fiction

MAMDT